C000025952

THE SEXY STRANGER

BOOK 1 - ITALIAN NIGHTS SERIES

JA LOW

Cover Design: Simply Defined Art

Updated Editor: More than words

Photographer: Wander Aguiar - www.wanderbookclub.com

Model: Valerio

❀ Created with Vellum

1

LILLY

It's been years since I've seen snow—fluffy white flecks fall to the ground in front of my car, creating a blanket of white over everything it touches—or the rock walls that line the narrow, winding country roads. The farmers' cottages that dot the usually emerald green hills now blend into the stark white countryside. The swirling smoke from their chimneys is the only way to see where each one is located.

Not much daylight filters through during these winter months. The last of the sun's rays set over the area's famous mountains, 'The Three Sisters of Glencoe,' nestled in the tourist trail of the Scottish Highlands. My sister and I explored these mountains as children, running through the green fields, picking thistles and field flowers for Nan, and jumping through streams that cut into the land from the snowy peaks surrounding us, freezing our toes if we slipped and fell in.

Our summers were spent helping around the farm—we fed the sheep, milked the cows and goats, and picked up the eggs from the chicken coop. Scottie, Nan's Scottish Terrier, would chase the chickens around the yard every time we'd collect the eggs. It would have us in fits of giggles watching the feathers fly.

A tear falls down my cheek remembering the old days. It's been a while since things have felt happy around here. It simply hasn't been the same since Nan died. We loved visiting her every school holiday, enjoying our freedom, which is a far cry from the hustle and bustle of London where we normally resided.

Our parents are world-renowned surgeons, working for London's elite at their famous Harley Street practice. Because of their dedication to medicine, and pretty much everyone else, they didn't have much time for us girls. Luckily, when we weren't with Nan, we had an eccentric Italian nanny named Contessa. She wore bright, vibrant colors, and was a loud, passionate woman who taught us to cook and speak Italian. She immersed us into her culture, one we still love to this day.

Contessa was obsessed with the British royal family, loved everything about it, so much so she'd wear a crown. She thought because her name means countess in Italian, that she must have been switched at birth and was actually royal. She used to have us in fits of laughter with her made-up tales of royal life.

A sad smile falls across my weary face remembering her. It was a shock when she passed at such a young age. She may be gone, but never forgotten. I wipe the errant tears from my sleep-deprived eyes.

"Oh, shit," I scream as the car skids across the road in the icy conditions. My heart's racing a hundred miles an hour, my adrenaline has gone into overdrive. I've been stuck in the African desert for far too long—seems I've forgotten how to drive in these treacherous conditions.

Thankfully, I rented a Range Rover 4WD, so it will keep me safe on these hazardous roads. If I had gone with the little hatchback the clerk was trying to push onto me, I'd have ended up in some snowy ditch somewhere. Then I'd have had to call Broden, the local mechanic, to come rescue me, which also means Seonaid, his wife, would hear about my return to Glencoe by myself. And with that, by morning the whole village would know, and

I'd have busybodies popping in all day. If Broden had to tow me, I don't think I'd be able to show my face again in the pub because Wallace would make sure that nobody forgot the time Lilly ran off the road and needed help. They have long memories here. Believe me, it would keep them entertained for years.

The snow's falling heavier now, my car's headlights are the only stream of light stretching across the vast, dark emptiness, a solitary beacon winding its way through the valley's treacherous bends. I slow as I enter the village which is quiet for this time of night with the weather closing in.

The only lights on in the village are from the pub which never closes. Wallace would never dare shut his doors to his fellow villagers. His family has owned this pub for two hundred years, or something like that, and the doors have never been closed, not even when the English invaded. But I'm not entirely sure if the English ever got this far—it's hard to tell when they are pulling your leg.

I pass the pub, which means I'm not far from the cottage.

Finally, almost home.

Oh, how I've missed you. Nearly two years away, longer when you count university and my residency in London.

I can't wait to surprise my sister, Laura. She was devastated when I told her I couldn't get Christmas off this year. For sisters, we're close. I think it's because Mom and Dad were never around, so we only had each other. But, little does she know I was able to switch contracts with one of the other doctors, who had fallen in love with one of the peacekeepers. She couldn't extend her contract, and lucky for her, I still had six months left on mine, which meant voilà, contracts changed, and I was on the next plane out of there.

It's funny how determined you are never to follow in your parents' footsteps, and yet here you are, years later, traveling in the exact same shoes. I decided not to pursue becoming a specialist like them as I wanted to use my skills to help people who really need it. I wanted to make a difference, and that didn't go over too well in our household.

"No daughter of mine is going to Africa to work. She wasn't brought up like that." Those were my father's words when I told him I said no to a prestigious private hospital that offered me a high-paying job. He was so angry with me until my fiancé told them he was traveling with me, that he wanted to develop our life skills over there, and that it would look good on our resumes when we eventually did come home and took over his family's practice. My father thought it was the best idea in the world and was fully supportive of us. In the end, that didn't work out so well for me.

I wind my way up the long driveway to the cottage. It's pitch black all around except for tiny specks of light glowing from the houses that dot the inky dark surroundings. White smoke billows out of the cottage's chimney, twisting its way into the night sky.

Oh, how I've missed the smell of a good fireplace. The smoky, woodsy scent, and the crackling of the logs as they burn. Many nights were spent sipping hot cocoa in front of its warmth while reading a good book in my flannel pajamas with Scottie curled up on his mat in front, snoring away. Nan sitting there knitting us beanies and mittens like she did every single year.

My heart is bursting with excitement. I can't wait to do all those things with my sister this year. But secretly, I'm looking forward to a hot shower, soft bed, comfy pillows, and a huge, snuggly duvet.

Finally here, I jump out of the car, quickly grabbing my bag from the rear seat. I only have the one. You don't need much when you live in an African refugee camp and wear scrubs all day.

The cold air stings my face. It shocks me. I've forgotten how cold Scotland is in the middle of winter. Making a mad dash to the front door with my head down, protecting it from the howling wind, I turn the knob knowing out here no one locks their doors, and push through. Instant warmth hits me as I shake off the remnants of the snow from my coat. I drop my bag on the wooden floor of the foyer, then hang up my winter jacket onto the hook. Rubbing my hands together, my skin comes back to life quickly as feeling returns to my fingers.

I close my eyes and take in the smell of the log fire, the smoke almost tickling my nose. I inhale deeply, taking me back to a time when life wasn't so damn complicated. My eyes open, and I expect to see my sister, Laura, rush out and greet me. What I wasn't expecting was a stranger—a sexy stranger at that—who's standing in my childhood home, naked.

I take him in.

All of him in.

Oh my.

Wow.

That is impressive.

2

LILLY

"Who the hell are you?" His deeply accented voice echoes through the cottage vibrating deep down into my bones and most certainly my lady bits. The white towel that he was using to dry his dark, almost black hair drops to the floor in surprise.

My eyes can't seem to stop scanning every inch of his amazing body, from the deep olive skin down over each perfectly cut muscle sculptured like some kind of renaissance masterpiece. Are men supposed to look like this? Because I have never seen any so perfectly made before.

My eyes travel further over him, down, down, down to ….

Okay, um, what does one do with something like that? I mean, I've seen dicks before, I'm a doctor, but this one is well, wow. It's the most beautiful cock I've ever seen, and we all know there are some ugly dicks out there. But when you stumble upon a prized beast like this, you have to take your time to admire it—this dick deserves admiration. I bet women make a sacrifice to the dick gods when he unwraps himself.

It's the perfect length. Not too big, not too small, just the right amount of girth, too. Meaty enough to fill you up, but not too much that you think you're being split in two. There's a nice even color tone with the perfect amount of veinage. Even his balls are impeccably symmetrical. No one has fucking perfect balls. No one. And, of course, he manscapes. This man cares for his lady friends, he understands what happens when a stray makes an appearance.

That reminds me, I have an Amazonian jungle covering my lady garden at the moment. I think it might be time for me to trim the hedges.

Stop it, Lilly, my inner good girl yells at me. *The way you're looking at him is sexual harassment.*

She's right, so very right, but I'm finding it really, really hard to look away.

I've been suffering a long-extended man drought, and now this tall drink of water is standing before me, and I'm thirsty.

Stop it. He's a stranger, a sexy one but a stranger nonetheless.

I'm blaming jetlag for my brain being completely shut down in this moment.

"Scusa ..." he clears his throat, "... my eyes are up here."

"I know ... I was just enjoying the view." My hands rush to my mouth, but the words are out before I realize what I have said.

What the hell has gotten into me?

The hot stranger's mouth twitches with a smile, but he recovers, keeping his face neutral.

Where the hell is Laura? Why would she have a naked guy in her home?

Did she break up with Andy?

No, they're so good together, they have been dating forever.

"Who the hell are you? Where's Laura?" I ask, looking around the room, hoping she'll jump out and surprise me, and that this handsome guy hasn't just murdered my family.

He frowns. "Laura?"

That accent is killing me. Italian. I have a weakness for accents. I mean, who wouldn't when there's a Roman god standing in front of you?

"I don't know a Laura."

Then who the hell is he?

"I'll ask you again, who the hell are you? And you better tell me the truth, or I'm calling the police and having you arrested for trespassing."

"Are you serious?"

"Damn right, I am. And heads up, I have a black belt. So, I'll kick your ass if you come anywhere near me," I warn him.

"Have you escaped the mental institution? Should I be worried?" he asks, his dark brows pulling together.

"I'm not crazy, you're the one who has broken into my home."

"No, I haven't. I'm renting this place."

"This is my house, and I can assure you I haven't rented it out to anyone," I argue.

"It's in my phone, the details. Let me get it," he says, waving his hands in the air to show me that's what he is grabbing. Unfortunately, that exposes his hot cock again and I take another look to make sure he's not about to attack me with a weapon. *Unless it's that weapon of a dick.* Lilly, cool it. You've lost your mind.

"Fine." My eyes narrow on him, but he seems genuinely confused by the whole situation, and my sister does have some hair-brained schemes sometimes, so I wouldn't be surprised if she rented out my room to someone.

He turns on his heel and heads down the hall. I take a look at his toned ass as he walks away. Nice, tanned buns. He must sunbathe naked to get an all-over tan like that.

Focus, Lilly.

I grab my phone out of my purse and call Laura. "Come on … pick up." But the phone rings out. I send her a text asking her to call me ASAP.

The beautiful cocked man comes out in a long-sleeve white T-shirt and gray sweatpants. Such a shame covering up a thing of beauty like that, but I can see he didn't add any underwear because the dick print is pushing hard against the material. *Nice.*

He flicks through his phone and then turns it to me. "The email is from Lolly."

My eyes scan down the email that says he's booked into my home for the next month.

I'm going to kill my sister! Where the hell is she?

"Lolly is my sister's nickname. We're Lilly and Lolly. Where the hell is my sister?" Handing his phone back to him I continue, "I can't believe she did this to me. This is *my* home. I … this was meant to be a surprise." I sit in one of the armchairs beside the fire feeling a little woozy with all this excitement.

"Lolly is your sister?" I nod. "The email says she was going away."

I nod again, but I'm not really listening to him. All I want is my bed, but it looks like he's staying in that room. Tears start to fall down my cheeks as the shock of everything going to custard kicks in.

"Signora, please." He sounds like he's unsure of what to do when a strange woman crashes his holiday, stares at him naked, then starts crying.

I mean, surely this happens all the time, right?

"I'm sorry. I just … I've just flown in from Kenya."

His chocolate eyes widen in surprise.

"I have nowhere to go … my sister was supposed to be here. It's snowing heavily outside. I nearly skidded off the road. I'm sorry to ruin your holiday. I had no idea she wouldn't be here." I sniffle.

The handsome man keeps his distance—probably smart.

"I'll go in the morning. Please, let me stay tonight. I can't go out there again."

He frowns a little but eventually nods.

"I'll just go into the other room." Pointing to the room across the hall. "That's my sister's."

He smiles, but it doesn't quite reach his dark, chocolatey eyes.

Grabbing my bag, I walk into my sister's room, the faint smell of her perfume lingering in the air. I fall onto the soft bed and scream into the pillow. *Where the hell is she?*

I must fall asleep at some point because I'm awakened by my phone ringing. Jumping up, I quickly grab it and notice it's Laura.

"Where the hell are you?" I scream into the phone.

"Um ... where the hell are you?"

"Excuse me ... I'm here in your bed, and there's a fucking stranger in mine." I raise my voice.

"What the hell are you doing in Scotland?"

"I've come home. It's a long story, one that I want to tell you in person, not over the phone. Where are you?"

Laura bursts out laughing.

I don't think any of this is funny. At all.

"Andy and I decided to come and surprise you ... in Kenya."

The world stops.

Did she just say Kenya?

"You're seriously not in Africa, are you?" My brain is computing the words she's saying, but I'm not really understanding because, seriously, this can *not* be happening.

"Yeah, we're standing right here with Rob. He seems very confused that you've disappeared suddenly. What's going on, Lil?"

I shake my head, the tears falling instantly, thinking about that man.

"Lil. Come back," I hear Rob call down the phone.

"Laura. Please, don't hang out with Rob," I plead with my sister.

"Hold on …" The voices in the background become fainter. "What's going on?"

"He's the reason I'm halfway across the world," I say with my hands shaking thinking about the bullshit story Rob is probably telling them.

"What the hell did he do?" My little sister is tiny, five-foot-two at best, but she is feisty. She always looked out for me even though she's two years younger.

"I've caught him numerous times screwing around with the nurses." Tears fall freely now, and it feels good to finally be telling someone.

"Oh, babe, I had no idea."

"I tried to keep it in, deal with it myself because I was stuck there. I had signed on for two years, and I couldn't break the contract, plus, I loved being there. I loved helping. Thankfully, one of the other doctors has fallen in love and wanted to stay, so we swapped. It was last minute, and I didn't have time to tell you. I didn't want Rob to know anything about me leaving, so I had to go."

Being stuck in the middle of nowhere with a cheating partner is hell. The first time I busted him, I'd woken up because it was so hot that night that I couldn't sleep. I stumbled from my bed and out into the night, the light breeze cooling me ever so slightly. I heard some strange noises around the corner of my tent and went to investigate. That's when I saw Rob screwing one of the nurses up against some boxes. She was this beautiful, sexy French nurse, who had been flirting with Rob ever since we had arrived, but I never thought for one minute he'd cheat on me.

I thought the diamond ring on my finger gave me security. I was wrong.

This is when I should've made a scene, screamed and yelled at him, told him what a horrible asshole he was, but I didn't. Instead, I turned around and made my way to the food tent to grab a bottle of water where I sat and cried by myself. Then I trudged back to my tent and went to sleep. Pathetic, really. I pretended the next day as if nothing had happened, not because I thought it was okay, but because I was stuck.

A couple of other times, late at night, I stumbled upon him, and each time it chipped away at my soul. I never said a word, that good old English stiff upper lip came in handy.

I simply waited for a chance to leave, and when it did, I took it.

I messed around on Rob once too. So, I guess I'm not so innocent, but it was after the fifth nurse when I just couldn't take it any longer. This gorgeous Canadian peacekeeper came into the camp—he was my new escort around the villages. While we were out, a huge storm started to brew, and we were too far away to safely make it back to camp in time. We had to wait it out in a tiny hotel room in the city. After a couple of drinks, I told him about Rob. How I had caught him one too many times fooling around on me, and that I was waiting patiently until my tenure was over and I could leave and never look back.

The next thing I knew, his lips were on mine, and we ended up in bed together. Not going to lie, it was amazing. It felt like a big 'fuck you' to Rob.

Once I got back to camp, I felt guilty even though I shouldn't have because Rob was most definitely not feeling guilty about his hook-ups. It was the one and only time for me, I never did it again.

"You bastard," Laura screams down the phone, pulling me from my memories. "You fucking bastard. How could you cheat on her?"

I can hear Rob trying to defend himself from Laura's onslaught.

"Lolly … Lolly … stop! Lol …." I'm trying to catch her attention, but it's as if she's dropped the phone.

"Lil." Andy picks up the phone.

"She's making a scene, isn't she?"

"Yeah, and to be fair, Rob's acting like a pussy, telling her he doesn't know what she's talking about. That he never cheated."

My eyes roll so hard—the damn coward.

"But Lolly isn't backing down. Oh, shit! I think security's coming. Gotta go. Will call you if we don't get arrested." And with that, he hangs up the phone.

I stare up at the wooden ceiling of the cottage, hundreds of years' worth of structure, and I laugh. I laugh and laugh until my stomach hurts. I can just imagine my little pocket rocket of a sister slapping and hitting Rob, where she can reach, that is, and him trying to protect himself from her. I love my sister so much. The fact she has flown halfway across the world to surprise me means everything, but even more so that she's defending my honor.

Moments later, my phone rings again.

"Lolly ... are you okay?"

"Yeah, I am. But Rob isn't." She sniggers. "I kind of caused a scene, and, well ... told everyone he works with he's a cheating scumbag. That my sister's way too good for him ..."

I let out a loud laugh.

"At least now everyone knows. They were all sad to see you'd left. You're very much loved here," she tells me.

I tear up again. "I know ... I miss them all so much as well," I state, thinking about the amazing villagers who had become my family while I was there.

"Did you say earlier you were in my room?" Laura asks.

"Yeah."

"Shit. Um ...."

"I've already met the person renting out the house. I kind of stumbled in on him naked."

"Oh my god, did you have to bleach your eyes?" My sister giggles.

"The total opposite, I couldn't stop staring. He's hot!"

Laura squeals down the phone. "This is fate, Lil. Fate."

Laura is the opposite of me. She believes in fate, soulmates, and happiness. She's a hairdresser and spends her days dressed in bright, colorful clothes with rainbow hair. She's dating Andy, a farmer here in Glencoe. They've been dating for a long while now, but he still hasn't put a ring on it. Not that she minds.

"You know I don't believe in fate."

"Well, tell me this. Why the hell am I here in Kenya and you're there in Glencoe? Both of us surprising the other for Christmas."

I love her enthusiasm for fate, but I'm a doctor. I think in logic and science. "Miscommunication, definitely not fate."

She scoffs at me. "No. Something's happening. Fate is up to something. She's sent a hot guy to our cottage, and you turn up after getting your heart broken."

"Hot Italian guy," I add.

"Oh my god, see ... you speak Italian, Lilly. See ... fate."

"Let's forget about fate for the moment. What the hell are we going to do now we're both on opposite sides of the world?" I ask her.

"Well, Andy's never been overseas, so I want to show him around," she says excitedly.

Selfishly I want her home, but the fact she got Andy halfway across the world is a miracle, so I can't take that away from her. She's been badgering him for years to go traveling, but he likes his simple life here in the mountains.

"I'm going to miss you, but you need to explore that beautiful continent. I'll see you when you get home."

"You sure?" Lolly asks.

"Yes. I'll be okay. I miss you so much. But Kenya is beautiful, and I can't wait for you to see all of it. I'll email you where to go and what to see in the morning."

"Thanks, babe. I'm so bummed we missed you. But I'm glad I kicked Rob's ass. I never liked him."

This makes me laugh because it's true. Laura's always

thought he was this rich, entitled snob who thought he was so much better than everyone else. Looking back now, she's right.

"Okay, well, have fun, send me loads of pics, and I love you," I tell her.

"Love you, too, sis. And jump that Italian Stallion."

"Bye, Lolly."

I fall back asleep quickly, jetlag taking over, and my heart feeling a little less broken.

3

LUCA

The smell of bacon and eggs pulls me from my sleep. Last night's unexpected visitor comes back into my memory, and the way she hungrily looked at me, not going to lie, I liked it. The blatant way she looked at my dick with appreciation—major turn-on. I liked that she was confident enough in herself to do that. She has a beautiful face, almost heart-shaped with big, expressive, bright blue eyes and plump lips. Her cheeks were pink from the cold. She appeared au naturel—her face free of any makeup. Tiny laugh lines crinkled at the side of her eyes, and frown lines were drawn across her forehead. She's most definitely all-natural, a huge difference from the women I'm normally seen with.

Then she threatened to call the police on me, and all sexiness faded away really fucking quickly. I don't need trouble with the law at the moment because once they run my name through the system, my safe little sanctuary will be ruined.

I'm not ready to face anyone just yet.

"Morning," I say, greeting her warily.

Lilly, I think that's the name she said last night, is dressed in an oversized white shirt and leggings as she moves around the small kitchen, her light brown hair is pulled up into a messy ponytail. Turning around with a black spatula in her hand, I'm greeted by her nipples staring right at me. Maybe she doesn't realize how see-through her T-shirt is because I can see the curve of her bare breasts straight through it.

Stop looking, Luca.

Actually, no. She took her time to look me over last night, I'm only repaying the favor.

"I just wanted to say how sorry I am for last night." She waves the spatula in the air. "I was really jet-lagged." She smiles. "I don't normally act like that." Her eyes look down at my pants as if to say, 'I don't normally check out men's dicks so openly.'

I can tell you now, no man will ever make you apologize for checking out their dick. No man.

When our eyes meet again, she seems flustered and waves the spatula nervously in the air as her cheeks burn bright red.

"Please accept a hot breakfast as my apology."

I give her a genuine smile. Honestly, I don't think a woman has ever made me breakfast that wasn't one of my staff.

"Grazie," I say. Taking the plate from her hand, our fingers connect for the briefest of moments, and a tiny zap travels through my body. She felt it too as her hand moves away from mine quickly like it burned her. I take a seat at the kitchen table and take in what's on my plate—it's filled with bacon, eggs, mushrooms, tomato, spinach, and a couple of slices of toast.

Was all this in my fridge? I don't remember seeing any of it. I know there was stuff in the fridge, but I guess I didn't take in exactly what was there. Once I grabbed the Scottish whisky, I decided on a liquid dinner instead last night.

She follows behind me, placing a bottle of water and juice in the middle of the kitchen table. "Would you like coffee?"

"Oh, no … No. No." That was a mistake I made when I first arrived, tasting the horrendous instant coffee sitting on the shelf.

I could kill for some real Italian coffee, but I don't think I'm going to find any here.

She laughs. "Of course, Italians would never drink instant."

Does she recognize me?

"How do you know I'm Italian?"

"My nanny was Italian. She spoke to us mainly in Italian, so I've picked up on some of the words you use." She takes a seat far away from me with her breakfast.

"So, you speak Italian?"

"I used to be fluent, but it's been a while since I've used it." She smiles through a mouthful of toast.

We both fall into silence as we eat our breakfast. I didn't realize how hungry I was until I started eating, and it doesn't take me long to finish it.

"There's more in the pan." She flicks her head in the direction of the kitchen.

I stare at her for a couple of beats then realize she means I have to get it myself.

Welcome to the real world, Luca.

I'm so used to people looking after me that I've never been self-sufficient. I grab some more bacon and make some more toast.

"I'm going to grab my bag and get out of your hair," she tells me, placing her plate in the sink.

Now she's in my space I'm not sure I want her to go. Not because I think she's cute, which I do—I certainly don't need a cute complication in my life at the moment—but honestly, I don't think I'm going to enjoy my own company. I had most of yesterday by myself, and it was so damn hard. I had to get drunk to even hang out with myself. For the next month, my only companion is probably going to be my whisky bottle, and I think I like the distraction standing in front of me much better.

"I heard there's a snowstorm coming. Is it safe for you to go?"

Her eyes widen. "Shit. Is there?" She grabs her phone and furiously taps away on it. "Bugger, you're right. They have issued a weather warning. I better go."

"Don't," I say, stilling her. "I couldn't forgive myself if something happened to you."

Lilly frowns at me. "I can't crash your holiday."

"I can't let a woman go out into a snowstorm."

Her hands go to her hips, and she looks a little angry. "But you'd let a man?"

Huh, what?

"I ... just ..." I stumble over my words.

"Exactly. Thank you, but I must be going." She looks like she can't wait to get away from me, and it's the exact opposite of how she looked at me last night. Maybe I was drunk and dreamed the whole situation. I guess that could be a distinct possibility. She picks up her bag and hauls it to the front door, stopping to pull on her coat and scarf. "Well, I hope you enjoy your stay here ..." her words trail off.

"Luke, my name is Luke." Technically, that is true, but she doesn't need to know any more. It's not like I'll be seeing her again.

"Luke." She smiles, saying my name, and I like hearing it across her lips. "Well, I hope you enjoy the cottage, it's truly a beautiful place." And then with that, she's gone.

A couple of moments later, the door suddenly opens, and I'm caught still staring at the space she vacated. "Sorry, I left the breakfast cleaning up for you but, you know, the storm and all." She waves at me and then closes the door again.

Maybe it's for the best, cuddling up to a cute girl isn't what I need. The distraction would be nice, but I must focus on the complete shitshow that's my life at the moment, away from everyone who wants to influence it.

Not long later, there's a knock at the door.

Who on earth could this be?

I move and open it, and swirls of snow hit me in the face, the wind is so fierce out there. Bright yellow lights on a tow truck flash through the white abyss.

"Hi …" Lilly moves from the side and into my view. "Guess you were right. You shouldn't have let a woman go out in the storm."

My heart stops. Is she hurt?

"Aye, he was, Lilly. Ye know not to go out in weather like this." A hulking giant places her bag on the doorstep. His eyes narrow on me, and he doesn't look happy. "Who's that, Lassie?" the man asks.

"This is Luke, a family friend." The man eyes me suspiciously. "He's Contessa's nephew over from Rome."

This seems to relax the old man a little. I wonder who Contessa is?

"God rest her soul."

Lilly appears sad at his condolence. She must have been close with this Contessa.

"Say hi to your wife for me," Lilly says, putting a large smile on her face when she bids him farewell.

He nods and disappears into the white.

Lilly lets out a heavy sigh, grabs her bag, and walks back into the cottage. "I'm sorry to be crashing your holiday, again."

"Are you okay?"

She shrugs. "Just a bruised ego more than anything. Slid off into a snowbank. That was Broden, he owns the mechanics shop in the village. Won't take long for the village grapevine to kick in and know that I'm back." She shucks off her jacket and hangs her scarf, then rubs her hands together. "I promise I won't be in your way. I'll lock myself in my sister's room until the storm has passed and let you holiday in peace."

"It's fine. Honestly, one day of my own company, and it was driving me crazy."

She laughs. "Not used to your own company, then?"

I shake my head. "I come from a big family. They like to get into my business. A lot."

"Sounds very Italian."

"It is," I agree which makes me smile thinking about my family for the first time since …. Shaking my head, I'm not going to think about it. I've messaged my brother to tell him I'm okay but I am requesting time by myself to get everything in order. I just hope they understand.

"They mean well."

Lilly smiles. "Family always does. I only have my sister who cares, and she's enough trouble as it is."

"Lolly?"

"Yeah, and I'm Lilly." She holds out her hand to me. "If I've forgotten to introduce myself in the chaos, I can't remember."

I take her hand and shake it—there's that zap of electricity again.

"Come sit, you're frozen," I say, feeling her cold hand. I usher her to one of the armchairs by the fire.

"Thanks," she says, giving me a wide smile as she rubs her hands together in front of the fire. I head into the kitchen and grab the bottle of whisky and two glasses, setting them down in front of the fire on the side table.

"That's Macallan whisky," she states, looking up at me with surprise.

"It's nice," I respond as I start pouring the amber liquid into the glasses.

"But … that's an expensive bottle."

I hand her the glass, and she stares at me.

I shrug. Shit. Did I just give myself away with the whisky? I could just be some busy executive needing time away to decompress. Yes, that's what I'll say.

"It was a Christmas present … from work."

"Work must really like you. That's a four-hundred-dollar bottle of whisky."

"I'm a hard worker." It's true, I do work hard, it never stops. That is until now when I have to hide away in the Scottish Highlands.

"Well, cheers to you and your hard work," she says, raising her glass. We clink the crystal together and take a sip. "This is so smooth," Lilly says, licking her lips.

The action is damn distracting.

"Hmmm …"

4

LILLY

This whisky is delicious. I haven't had alcohol in such a long time that I can feel it going straight to my head. My body is warm. I pull my feet up underneath me and rest my head back against the chair listening to the crackling of the fire.

"So, you were in Africa?" Luke asks.

"Yeah, I'm a doctor or … was a doctor. Guess I'm kind of unemployed now that I've just upped and left."

"Why?" he asks.

I watch as he takes another sip of his whisky, his plump lips pressing against the glass. Holy shit, that's hot. I guess six months of forced celibacy sends you man crazy.

"It's a long story …." I groan.

"I'm not going anywhere. We're kind of stuck in a snow-storm." Luke smiles, but it quickly fades when he sees my face. "But it's not any of my business."

Should I tell this sexy stranger about my messed-up relation-ship, or will that put him off?

Seriously, Lilly, you're not going to sleep with this man. It's probably unethical or something seeing as he's paid your sister to stay at your home. But he's so hot.

"I think I'm going to need more liquor for this story …." I laugh, hoping to mask the sadness.

"Oh, it's one of those. Hold on …" he says as he jumps up, runs to the kitchen, and looks through the cupboards. There's a lot of clanging and banging until he appears with a beautiful cheese platter and a bottle of bubbly.

"Are you a magician or something?" I ask, not sure where he pulled that from.

"It was in the fridge. We should probably line our stomachs first," he says.

"Good idea," I agree as he pops the bottle.

"This is from a friend's vineyard. It's Trento DOC, an Italian sparkling wine. Tastes like prosecco, but this is found in the vineyards of the Trentino-Alto Adige region. That's where the Dolomites are which make up part of the Italian Alps."

"Not as majestic as the Alps, but we have mountains here that loom over the town like the Alps do. Tourists come to walk them in the summer."

"Si, I have not had a chance to look around yet. Maybe when the storm has settled, you could show me … be my guide," he suggests.

My cheeks warm at his invitation, and my lips turn up into a smile. "Sure, if you're not sick of me by then."

He hands me a glass and grins. "I think your company might be better than my own." This makes me laugh. "The reason this wine is called Trento DOC is because the capital of the region is called Trento, and DOC is the name of the official Italian wine-naming system."

"You seem to know a lot about your friend's vineyard."

"I've listened to him so many times talking about it, I guess it has sunk in," he says, giving me a wide smile.

"I think having a friend who owns a vineyard would be a

great friend to have because this wine is delicious," I say as the bubbles tickle my nose.

"I'll pass on your critique when I see him next. He'll be very happy a beautiful woman likes his wine."

Did he just call me beautiful?

Luke obviously understands his mistake and quickly covers his words. "So, tell me what happened in Africa that made you want to surprise your sister?"

I take a big sip of wine to calm my nerves. "My fiancé thought sleeping with the nurses in the camp was a good idea." Luke chokes on his drink, and I continue, "Yep, and stupidly, I let him. Never said a word."

"Why not?"

"Because I was stuck in the African desert. I had signed a contract, and I couldn't leave. I … I felt trapped and a long way from home. I didn't know what to do. I thought it would be easier if I ignored it."

"How were you able to continue every day as if nothing had happened? That seems soul-destroying. How were you able to forgive him?"

I can hear the questioning tone in his voice. "Just because I ignored it doesn't mean I forgave him. After the first time, I stopped sleeping with him. I changed my shifts, made sure I was always busy, and pushed him away. He didn't care. He never once questioned me why we were never together. Why we never slept with each other."

"I'm sorry."

"Yeah, so am I. I wasted years with someone who wasn't interested in me. Honestly, I don't think I ever loved him or he me."

A twenty-four-hour flight gives you some perspective about your life when all you have is time to think about it.

Twirling the glass in my hand, I continue, "Our parents were friends through work, all great surgeons in their fields. They

pushed us together, hinted that the merging of the two families'
practices would be beneficial, and that we could take it over once
we returned from Africa. They had our lives all mapped out
for us."

"Did he think this was his last chance before he settled
down?" he asks.

"Probably, maybe, who knows? He knew I wouldn't kick up
a fuss if I found out because of my family. I was far more
worried about disappointing my parents than I was about him
disappointing me."

"I understand that," Luke says quietly.

"Grown-ass adults, and we still worry about what our parents
think." I huff.

Luke smiles and raises his glass to cheers me. Good to know
someone else has a complicated history with their parents too.

"So, you never ..."

Typical male, wondering how on earth you could go without
sex for so long.

"Once. I met a lovely Canadian soldier who I was showing
around. We got caught in a storm and had to find a hotel somewhere. And one thing led to another and ..."

"You seem to like getting caught in storms with strange
men." Luke chuckles as he looks at me over his glass.

Is he flirting with me? I blush under his gaze. "My sister
calls it fate."

"Fate?" Luke raises his brows at the word.

"Yes, she thinks ... oh my god, I need to shut up. This wine
is going to my head. Never mind," I say, waving my hands at
him. Stop embarrassing yourself in front of this hot man.

"What, no, you must continue. Your sister thinks ... what?"
he asks.

I roll my eyes. "Lolly thinks running into you at the cottage
is fate."

His eyes widen at that remark.

"See, you think I'm crazy."

"I think I told you last night I thought you were." He smirks at me.

I bury my face into the armchair, utterly embarrassed. "Ugh, I'm still so sorry about last night. About the whole … you know …" I wave my hand in his dick's general direction.

"Checking out my dick?" He fills in the blanks for me as his accent caresses the words making them sound dirty.

How on earth does the word 'dick' sound so sexy from his mouth and not creepy like it usually does when other guys say it?

"I understand now. It's been a while. You were only human. It's impressive … no?" he teases.

I pick up the cushion behind my head and throw it at him playfully. It knocks the glass of wine in his hand and spills it all over his white T-shirt.

Fuck.

"I'm so sorry." That was so stupid, Lilly. What the hell do you think you're doing? No more wine for you.

But Luke surprises me and slowly starts peeling the soaked T-shirt off his body.

My teeth sink into my bottom lip as my pulse starts beating out of time, warmth washes over my skin, and a tingle settles between my legs.

No, no, no … this is bad.

"What are you doing?" I squeak out as my cheeks burn brightly.

"Taking off my shirt," he says as if it's no big deal he's getting half naked with me again.

To be fair, you've already seen the Full Monty. What's a half monty?

My chest becomes heavy as I try to swallow while my mouth turns dry.

"But … you can't sit there without a shirt," I question, waving my hand furiously in front of him.

"Why? Will you not be able to keep your hands off me?" He smirks.

Jerk.

Even if there is some slight truth to that. He doesn't need to spell it out like that. The man's chest is a thing of beauty— tanned, toned, a little glossy from a sheen of sweat settling over his skin from sitting close to the fire.

Shut it down, Lilly.

Right now!

"As if. I'm not desperate," I reply, rolling my eyes which only serves to make him laugh.

"The flushed cheeks tell me otherwise."

"That's from the wine. Most definitely not from you," I bite back. *It's most definitely from him.*

"Are you sure about that?"

What a cocky bastard. *The man is hot, of course he's cocky.*

"Of course I am."

"Last night says differently," he says, raising a brow.

"I was jetlagged and confused."

"You couldn't keep your eyes off my dick," he teases.

"That's because I was in shock at finding a naked man in my home."

"Wasn't because it's been a while?" he pushes.

"Excuse me?"

"When was the last time someone touched you, admired you, satisfied you?" he questions me.

My mouth falls open. "You stop that right now. Stop it with that Italian sex voice. I'm sure it works on hundreds of ladies, but it's not going to work on me. Yes, you're a very good-looking man. I'm sure you know this because you own a mirror, but do not assume because I haven't had sex in six months ..." his eyes widen at my statement, "... that I'm some easy prey for you. I'm not one of those girls."

"Six months?"

That's what he's stuck on? "Of course, that's what you focus on. Yes, it's been six months, and I don't see that ending anytime soon." I glare at him. "When was the last time you had sex?" I ask, crossing my arms in front of me defensively.

"A week ago."

Of course, look at him. He probably has a different woman each night. "Ugh ... men," I reply while throwing my hands up in the air. I stand and walk into the kitchen, grabbing myself a glass of water to cool down.

"Please, tell me you self-love," he yells from the living room.

I still. *He didn't just ask me that.* Turning around quickly, I stalk toward him, stabbing my finger into his hard chest. "Of course, I do, and it's so much better than any orgasm any man has ever given me."

"Then you have been with the wrong men." Those chocolate eyes look up at me, and that cocky smirk infuriates me.

"And guess what? There's no way in hell you're going to be the right one, either. Good night, Luke." I turn on my heel and stomp to my bedroom, slamming the door. I'm going to need some self-love after that exchange. Because Mr. Sexy Stranger has me hot under the collar.

5

LUCA

S tupido. Stupido. Stupido.

I pushed her out of her comfort zone. I took the flirting and joking too far, especially after the story she told me about why she left Africa. Her ex? He's a moron. Lilly is a fun, smart, feisty, easy-going, beautiful woman. She is so different from the women I usually date. I mean, she has a proper job for a start. She's a doctor. And the charity work she's doing isn't some gala put on by rich people. She's in there, hands-on with underprivileged people, making their lives better on the ground.

"Lilly," I whisper, knocking on her door. I need to apologize to her. I let the wine go to my head, and the craziness of the last couple of days might have caught up to me and made me act in a way I wouldn't normally. The door creaks open, and I see her eyes are a little red.

Shit, I've made her cry.

"Lilly … I'm …" But I don't get very far before she's pulling me into her, her lips touching mine in a frantic kiss.

I instinctively open for her, my hands finding her body and

pulling it flush against me. Our tongues duel, neither willing to give up control. Tiny mewls fall from her.

"Please, don't say a thing," Lilly says as she keeps kissing me, her hands roaming all over my bare chest. "Just, please ... don't speak."

My hands squeeze her ass through the thin material of her leggings. "Not even if it's to tell you that I want to pick you up and lay you down on your bed, strip you out of your clothes ..."

"Nope." She continues kissing me as I pull her T-shirt over her head, throwing the offending material to the floor. Her lips are on me again before I get a chance to take in her naked torso.

"Not even to tell you that my lips and tongue want to kiss and lick every inch of your body, starting here ..." I suck on the delicate skin right under her ear, "... then moving along to here." I kiss along her collarbone to the other side of her neck where I let my teeth sink into her flesh, giving it a little nip. She lets out a moan. "Moving along further ..." My lips move down from her neck to the swell of her breast, kissing the rounded flesh before moving between her décolletage with my tongue, feeling the goosebumps break out all over her skin until I reach the other side. "Your nipples are aching with need. They are demanding to be touched, caressed, sucked, aren't they?" Looking up at her as my tongue laves the underside of her breast, her cheeks are pink with need.

"Yes," she answers on a whisper before closing her eyes and leaning back against the wall.

"Good girl." Moving over from the swell of her breast to her pert, needy nipple, I run my tongue along the outside of it while Lilly hums at the movement. Teasingly, over and over, I lick around the nipple not giving her what she needs until my teeth nip, and Lilly groans in appreciation. My hand caresses and kneads the other breast while my tongue drives her crazy.

"More ..." she pants.

Yes, Bella, I'll give you more.

Moving one of my hands lower until I reach her material-clad pussy, I let my fingers run along the seam pressing it against her aching clit making her hiss. I can feel her heat and wetness through her leggings.

She wants this.

Needs this.

And I'll give it to her.

Show her what real orgasms feel like. Let whatever this is be about her because she deserves that. I'm a giving man. I like to help where I can, and sex, well, that's my specialty. Reluctantly, I move from her breasts as I kiss down her taut stomach to the band of her leggings.

"These need to come off." My command is almost a growl as my fingers tug on the hem and roll them down her long legs, taking her underwear with them. Her hand instantly hides her pussy from me.

"*Open your legs,*" I tell her in Italian. Now isn't the time to be shy. Those bright blue eyes widen, and she hesitates for a few seconds but does what she's told. She's freshly shaven. Did she do this for me? No. I wish she'd thought of me as she freshened herself up. It's all pink and plump. Perfetto. Giving her one last heated look, she watches me as I move forward, grabbing her ass tightly, and pushing her harder against the wall. Then she watches with breathless anticipation as my tongue makes its first swipe between her folds and her eyes flutter shut.

"*You taste so good,*" I tell her as I savor her.

"Luke." Desire laces my name as it falls from her lips while her fingers thread through my hair.

My tongue slides between her folds again and again, and my nose is buried between her lips taking in her sweetness. She's so responsive, so wet. Letting go of one of her cheeks, my hand moves between her thighs. I add a thick finger, slowly sinking it into her heat. Lilly arches her back at the intrusion and moans. Slickness coats my finger as it slowly moves between her heat. I let my thumb catch her clit when my finger enters her. She tightens around me instantly. I add another finger, filling her as they move easily inside of her. Lilly's fingers are tightly threaded in my hair, and the pain is the perfect balance with the pleasure. She begins to contract around my fingers as I find the bundle of nerves that I know is going to set her off. Lilly is becoming wetter with each thrust inside of her.

"Have you ever been this wet before?" I ask, and she shakes her head. "I told you, you were with the wrong men."

"Yes." Nodding on a moan, my fingers curl inside.

"You deserve to be pleasured."

"Yes, yes, I do." She groans.

Her legs begin to shake, and she thrashes against the wall, but I never let up. She's close, so close. Her cheeks are flushed, and the color has crept down her neck and spread out across her chest.

"Luke, fuck ..." she curses as her orgasm catches her off-guard.

My fingers don't let up. I make her push through it because she deserves another one. Plus, in all honesty, my male ego has taken over, and I want to prove that I'm the best she has ever had, which probably isn't that hard because her ex sounds like a dick.

My fingers continuously curl inside of her as they concentrate on those sensitive nerves. "More, Lilly. I want more."

"No, I can't ..." She pants as her body begins to convulse again. "Luke, oh God ..."

I'm not God, but I sure as hell am going to make you feel like I am. A perfectly timed thumb against the clit has her seeing stars as she comes hard all over my hand. Her head is thrown back as she screams her release. Her chest is heaving, her face is flushed, and her blue eyes are bright and sparkling. She's glowing and never looked more beautiful.

"Did I?"

Feeling the wetness all over my hand, I reply, "Yes, Bella."

"I … I've never …." Lilly's hands come up and cover her face in embarrassment.

"No," my answer is commanding, and slowly she pulls her hands away from her face. "You'll never ever feel ashamed from satisfaction. You hear me?" My fingers are still inside of her, and reluctantly, I pull them from her while she watches my actions. They glisten in the late afternoon light, and one by one, I suck her off me. Those blue eyes widen in surprise, but I can see the desire behind them.

"Now, let me clean you up." Grabbing her leg, I place it over my shoulder.

"Luke?" she questions me.

"Lilly," I reply, staring back at her.

She bites her bottom lip nervously. Turning my head ever so slightly, I press a kiss against her soft, creamy thigh. Her teeth sink further into her luscious lip. Running my nose along the softness of her thigh until I find her open wide for me, I do exactly as I told her I'd do. I lick up every single bit of sweetness with my tongue until she's screaming out my name again. Her entire body shudders as the tiny orgasmic spasms take over, liquefying her legs, and she begins to sag against the wall unable to keep herself up any longer. I catch her before she hits the floor. Not going to lie, that's a pretty big ego boost making a woman come so hard she nearly collapses.

Lilly is limp in my arms as I place her gently on her bed, her head resting against the pillow, her eyes fluttering shut.

"Lilly …" I say her name, but all she can manage is a mumble of something incoherent. I hang my head, my dick groaning at the missed opportunity that's slowly disappearing.

I wish I were buried deep inside that gorgeous pussy as well, I tell my dick.

"Luca …" I still, my heart racing.

Did she just say my real name?

How?

"*Sleep,*" she says in Italian.

This is the first time I've heard her speak my mother tongue, and I like it. It's probably for the best that we didn't go any further, we're both full of complications. This was just an animalistic need brought on by whisky. That's it, whisky and wine.

Pulling back the duvet, I turn on my side and spoon Lilly with my arm wrapping around her. It's nice to feel wanted for me and not for who I am for once.

6

LILLY

A heavy arm is lying over me, and a large palm is cupping my breast in a familiar way. It takes me a couple of moments to remember where I am and who I'm with. I have no idea what time it is because it's dark, which it is most of the time here in winter. It could be one in the morning or three in the morning. Who knows? What I do know is Luke is sleeping soundly against me, with an enormous hard-on pressed into my back. That can't be comfortable.

Memories of what happened earlier in the afternoon return in all their technicolor, then I remember falling asleep after one too many orgasms. No wonder men fall asleep so quickly, one orgasm must feel like multiple for women.

Man, Luke's a dirty talker. I don't think anyone has ever dirty-talked me, or if they have, it was probably cringe-worthy, and I made them stop. But Luke, wow. Maybe it's the accent or maybe Italian men know how to sex a lady properly.

The way he teased my body was indescribable. No one has ever spent that amount of time on foreplay before. Usually, it's just a couple of licks or some finger bangs hoping you hurry up and get wet, so they can get their rocks off. But Luke, he just …

Shivers break out over my body remembering the way he lavished me. And what a gentleman as well, falling asleep right with me, even though he was probably beyond turned on and maybe a little miffed. Some guys would've woken me up and demanded that I finish them. I know for sure Rob would have.

My stomach turns just thinking about my ex. I know now that what I had with Rob wasn't love, it wasn't even damn lust. And to think I was going to marry that man and put up with a non-existent sex life. He most certainly wouldn't have had a non-existent one—he'd probably be out sleeping with every single woman he could find. Totally dodged a bullet there, even though I'm not looking forward to the conversation with my parents about why Rob and I are no longer together. I'm sure it will be all my fault, and I'll have brought shame across the family. They'll yell at me about how they won't be able to socialize with his parents anymore now we're not together.

No. Don't let them ruin your newfound singleness.

I turn and look at the stranger in my bed. This is so unlike me to have a one-night stand or whatever this is. I used to be a relationship kind of girl—four dates or more before you get sex. Now, this is the second one I've had. I have always followed the rules and look where that got me—a cheating fiancé, heartbreak, and a lifetime of trust issues.

Maybe I should think about throwing the rules out the window.

You kind of already have. That's right, I have.

I disappeared halfway across the world and ended up in bed with a hot Italian who gave me multiple orgasms. See what happens when you throw the rules out the window? Good things happen.

Rolling myself over in Luke's arms, I stop and stare at him. Totally creepy, I know, but it's the only chance I can get without it being weird. His dark hair floppily hangs over his face. My fingers itch to move it away, so I can look at him in all his glory. His square jaw sees the start of his five o'clock shadow.

Will I get another chance with him? Or was it a one-off mix of too much whisky and wine kind of thing?

Who's this man?

Why is he in the middle of the Scottish Highlands?

Why is he not with his family, especially an Italian family? I can't imagine they would be happy about him not being home for the holidays.

Is he single? My stomach drops for a moment. I didn't think about if he had a partner or not as I pulled him into my bed earlier.

Oh, shit. Shit.

"Are you watching me sleep?" Luke's voice makes me jump.

"No," I say quickly. His eyes are still closed.

"Feels like you are." A smirk falls across his lips.

"Are you single?"

His eyes open wide. "I'm no cheater, Lilly." His voice dips low at my question.

"I just …"

"I'd never have let it go as far as it did if I was." He sits up on one elbow, the white sheet falling, exposing his rippling chest.

Do not drool, Lilly.

"Just wanted to check because …" Heat falls across my cheeks as the thoughts swirling in my mind aren't voiced.

"Because what?" He seems genuinely curious.

Throw out the rules, Lilly!

"I was debating if I should wake you up or not to give you a blowjob." My words are out in a rush.

Luke chuckles beside me. "Never debate a blowjob. A blowjob is always a good idea. Always!"

Smiling back at him I think, *Make the move.*

So, I do as I'm told and push him onto his back and straddle him. "Good to know." I unabashedly rub myself against him. I notice he's taken off his jeans and left his boxer briefs on. At some point, he's put my underwear back on too. Why does that warm my heart?

Thick fingers dig into my ass as I move against his hardened cock.

"You don't have to do this." Luke looks at me, letting me know that he doesn't need the reciprocation.

"I want to." Pushing myself against him, I say, "I … I might suck at it, though."

Luke stills, his face is now serious. He reaches out and cups my concerned face. "As long as you're sucking, then it's all good."

My body relaxes a little at his joke. *You've got this, girl!*

"Well, then …." Leaning over and placing a kiss on his chest, my lips meet pure hardness as they make their way down every dip and plain of his body. Further and further I move down to the sweet spot. He's already standing at attention against the tightness of his boxer briefs. My fingers tug on the hem of his underwear, and they slide down. His cock springs to attention, nearly taking my eye out.

Be serious, Lilly. This is a serious matter. You're trying to be sexy. Sexy for the Italian Stallion. I internally groan using my sister's pet name for him.

I look back up to Luke who's now resting on both elbows, watching me.

How many girls have been in this same position? Hundreds probably, you only have to look at him. They are probably all porn-star worthy at giving head as well.

"Get out of that head of yours." Luke grins down at me. "I can hear the wheels turning all the way up here."

I close my eyes and die of embarrassment.

This isn't sexy at all.

Suck it up, Lilly. Ha, ha, you said suck it up when you really are about to suck it up.

"Is my dick amusing to you?" Luke raises a brow at me.

Oh damn, I was grinning at the stupid joke inside my head, and he thinks I'm making fun of his dick.

"No, your dick is perfection."

"Perfection, huh?" I can see his ego-inflating smirk now.

Good one, Lil, tell him more.

"That's what I thought last night when I saw you for the first time. You have one good-looking dick."

Luke bursts out laughing.

This wasn't how I saw my blowjob going.

"You have interesting dirty talk, Lilly, especially when my dick is out."

I look down at said object, which is staring right back at me. "When I'm nervous, I get the giggles and think crazy things in my head." I'm babbling, I know it. This isn't good.

Luke sits up and stares at me. "Lilly, you don't have to do anything you don't feel comfortable with. What we did earlier … was enough."

Urgh, why is he being so sweet? And what we did earlier was enough for me but not for him. Pull up those granny panties and take one for womankind and suck that dick like you're some kind of porn star. I'm trying to recall past PornHub videos I've watched on blowjobs when I was trying to impress Rob. Maybe I shouldn't have, they didn't seem to do the trick.

My head moves, and before Luke can say anything else nice to me, I have his dick firmly in my mouth.

"Oh, mio …" Luke falls back against the bed, and the groan that falls from his mouth is hot like he kind of likes it. I move my mouth up and down his shaft. "Bellissimo." I know that means beautiful, so I must be doing okay. Now I turn the suction on. "Fanculo."

Ah-huh swear words, that must mean he likes it, so I continue sucking him in, further and further down my throat. Holy cow, who knew I could deep throat? Hell, yeah, I'm totally taking him all the way back in my throat. This is awesome. I feel powerful, I feel alive, I feel like a woman. Great, now I have that Shania Twain song stuck in my head.

Oh, oh, oh ... man, I feel like a woman. I'm so lost in karaoke land that I've totally forgotten what the hell I'm doing, but the slew of Italian curse words coming from Luke's mouth, the way his eyes are closed, his back is arched, and his fingers are digging into the sheet, I know I'm a motherfucking porn star. "Oh, mio dio, *my god.*" Luke groans, and I'm so lost in being a porn star that I miss him tapping me on the arm. Ignoring him, I continue on. My hand cups his balls, which makes his toes curl, and he releases the deepest, wildest sound as a surprise hits the back of my throat.

Oh my god, he just came in my mouth.

I have never swallowed before.

I can't swallow this. It tastes gross.

Oh my god, I think I'm going to throw up. It's warm. *Eww.*

Everything happens in slow motion.

I spit out all over him.

Luke has just had the best blow of his life—*I'm totally calling it for him*—and I go and ruin it by spraying him with his own love juices. Luke's chocolate eyes widen as he looks down at himself, then up at me as I'm wiping my mouth. Some of it drips down my chin. *Eww.*

"Lilly, that was the biggest load I've ever blown." He looks at me in shock, then we both burst out laughing.

I always thought sex had to be serious until now.

Who knew it would be awkward and funny and a little bit messy?

7

LUCA

Not going to lie, that was one of the best and worst blowjobs of my life. Best, because that woman has a phenomenal mouth, and worst, because, well, my load ended up all over me. Next time, I'll know to be more forceful with my tapping. She seemed very lost in giving me head at the time. Thankfully, we were both able to laugh about it.

"I'm so sorry." Lilly looks up at me with those bright blue eyes.

"Not the ending I thought was going to happen." I notice a bit of me drip off her chin. That, right there is every man's dirty little fantasy.

"I …"

Lilly's embarrassed about it but starts laughing again.

"Next time I'll know to tap a little harder."

"Next time I might learn how to swallow."

She's thinking about a next time—I want there to be a next time.

"Um … so I might just go and clean up," she says. Jumping out of her bed, she hightails it into her bathroom, the door slamming shut behind her. The sound of the shower turns on, and I know that's my cue to leave. Pulling my underwear up, I grab my jeans and head back to my bedroom to grab a shower.

The warm water flows over me as memories of earlier filter back through my mind about how responsive she was to my tongue. I think Lilly's ex was some kind of selfish bastard, who wouldn't want to bring Lilly to her knees via his tongue. She's different from the other girls I've been with.

Honestly, I couldn't imagine any of the models or socialites to have laughed over our sexual mishap. No, they would've swallowed me down like pros and would have made a big song and dance over it too. Those girls think they are perfect, super-human even, they would've taken whatever I gave them and asked for more. But I'm coming to realize it's the dents and kinks in someone that makes them who they are. Having a flat, shiny surface loses its appeal after a while because they all end up looking the same.

It's refreshing.

No, Lilly is refreshing.

She is who she is and doesn't seem to apologize for it. She wears leggings and old T-shirts, her hair is pulled up in a messy, knotty ponytail. She doesn't wear a lick of makeup, yet she is one of the most beautiful women I've seen.

She can never be yours, Luca.

Ah, but she can be Luke's.

While I am here, I'm going to be Luke. Luke relaxes and has fun and doesn't worry about the consequences. He has no burdens, his life is great, uncomplicated. I want to be that man for Lilly.

"All clean?" Lilly asks as I walk into the kitchen, the delicious aromas filling my nose. The scene is oddly domestic, and I kind of like it.

"Yes. All clean." As I pass Lilly, I give her a kiss on the cheek and a tap on her bottom which makes her giggle.

"Who said you could touch me so freely?" She raises an eyebrow as I grab two beers from the fridge.

"Oh, sorry. I didn't realize it was a one-time kind of thing." Genuinely, I'm surprised. She looks away, flustered, as she stirs something in the pot.

"I ... just ... didn't think you would ... you know ..." she says nervously.

I want more time with her, especially in bed.

"You can have me for as long as you want," I tell her.

"For as long as the snowstorm has set in," she adds, trying to give us an end date.

Shaking my head, I'm being utterly selfish because she's taking my mind off things back home, and in all honesty, it's what I need at the moment.

"This snowstorm is going to be around for a while," I say, resting my hip against the kitchen bench. "This is your home. You should be able to stay and enjoy it." My answer surprises her as she stills what she is doing.

"I've crashed your holiday. It's not fair for you to pay and have a boarder with you."

"I don't care about the money." Her eyes widen at my answer.

"It's a lot of money."

I shrug. Money is no issue for me. I crack open the bottles of beer.

"No." Turning and glaring at me, she says, "I don't feel right about that. I'll ask my sister to refund your entire stay."

"What? No." I place the bottles of beer on the counter. "Lilly, don't worry about the money."

She keeps shaking her head. "It doesn't feel right."

"You're cooking a gorgeous dinner for me," I say, soaking in the smell. "If I were by myself, I'd be living on cheese and whisky for the entire month. So, you're really doing me a favor." Those blue eyes narrow trying to work me out. "I'm enjoying your company," I add, which makes her brow quirk up a little and a smile fall across her lips.

Picking up the bottle of beer, I hand it to her in a kind of peace offering way. She takes it from me, and I raise my bottle to hers. "To being stuck in a snowstorm." We clink our bottles and take a sip.

"So, Luke …" Lilly starts as she stirs the bubbling concoction in the pot. "Where do you come from?"

I knew she'd want to know more, especially if we're going to continue spending our time in each other's beds.

"Italy." Taking a nervous sip of my beer, Lilly rolls her eyes at me as she continues stirring. "I split my time between Roma and Firenze, sometimes Milano."

"Rome, Florence, and Milan?" she repeats, turning her head to look at me.

"Si." I take another sip of my beer.

"What do you do for a living, then? Those are some of the most beautiful cities in the world."

"I'm a businessman," I reply, leaving it pretty vague.

She eyes me suspiciously but decides not to press any further. "Do you mind setting the table? Dinner's almost ready."

Placing my beer on the table, I grab the cutlery from the drawers and move around setting the kitchen table.

Lilly brings over two large bowls and positions them on the table.

"I took a risk making Spaghetti Bolognese for an Italian, but it was quick and easy."

"You do know that Bolognese isn't technically Italian." My family would kill me if I didn't do my service preserving the Italian culture.

"I know. My nanny would kill me for serving this to you, but I like it."

"It smells delicious." The herbs and garlic aromas filter through my nose making my hunger pangs spike. "Plus, I've worked up an appetite." My heated words make Lilly stop mid-forkful and her cheeks turn a light shade of pink at my innuendo.

"Saluti." I hold up my beer.

Lilly places her fork back down in her bowl and holds up her beer bottle.

"Saluti." She cheers me back, then we both dig in.

"This is delicious," I say between mouthfuls.

"That means a lot coming from an Italian." She chuckles.

"Now, if you can find me some proper coffee, I might have to think about marrying you."

"Well, that's not going to happen around here. So, you better call off the priest now." We both laugh at the silly joke.

The conversation flows between us easily. She tells me about her childhood nanny and the crazy things they got up to. She also tells me about her nan and the fun times she had sitting in this cottage. This is a far cry from the privileged upbringing I had.

"Wanna play a game?" Lilly asks.

My brows rise. She's kinky as well? This girl is full of surprises.

"Get your head out of the gutter, Luke. I meant a board game."

I don't remember the last time I played a board game, or even if I have. "Um … sure."

"Don't look so scared. I promise to go easy on you." Lilly winks at me as she excitedly jumps up from the kitchen table and rustles in the hallway closet. She walks back with a dusty box and places it down on the table.

"Monopoly. What's that?"

"What?" she gasps. "You have never played Monopoly?" Lilly looks at me as if I'm some rare breed of alien.

"No. We didn't play board games in my family."

"Oh, my … I feel sorry for you. What kind of childhood did you have that there was no Monopoly?" she says it jokingly, but little does she know how rigid a life I grew up in. "It's one of the greatest games on earth. I thought you being a businessman and all that this would be right up your alley."

"Be warned, I'm a ruthless businessman, and I'll be an even more ruthless opponent," I tell her, taking my seat back at the table.

"Game on, then." She glares at me over the table.

"What? No. What do you mean I have to pay you rent? I don't have any money left," I exclaim, looking at the board.

"You have to sell everything. Pay or declare bankruptcy, and I win."

How on earth did this woman beat me at a game of real estate? "Take pity on me, woman. This is my first time."

"Hell, no. I'm one of the most competitive women you'll ever know. There's nothing you can offer me that will make me change my mind."

Challenge accepted.

I stand and walk around to her side, then start kissing her neck.

"Wh ... what are you doing?" Her voice is shaky.

"You said there was nothing in the world that would make you forfeit the game, and I'm testing this theory." My lips trail all over her skin while tiny goosebumps prickle under my lips.

"This is cheating, you know ..." her words trail away as my lips continue their assault.

"Or, I'm switching to a new game, one we both can win at."

She laughs. "That seems like a valid suggestion."

I walk around the chair and ask for her hand, which she gives me willingly. I pull her up and out of the chair, then throw her over my shoulder.

"Luke, Luke," she screams with delight, thumping my back.

Luckily, the cottage is small as I rush toward my room, kicking the door open and throwing her on the bed.

"You're crazy."

"I guess your crazy is rubbing off on me." I give her a wide smirk. I open the bedside table, pull out a condom, and throw it onto the bed. Her eyes widen at the action.

"Guessing the game is getting serious." Her eyes darken to an almost sapphire as she starts to undress, the timidness that she'd shown before now gone as she feels more comfortable in my company. Good.

I follow her lead and strip off my T-shirt and track pants. She throws her leggings at me, which makes me laugh. I settle myself over Lilly, hovering enough that I don't squash her.

"You were a pleasant surprise."

She smiles up at me. "So were you."

The moment settles between us, both of us surprised at the ease we find ourselves in, seeing as we're very much strangers, but at this moment in time, I feel like I can be myself and not the person my family wants me to be.

No responsibility.

No pressure.

No pretending.

Just me.

Slowly, I nudge at her entrance, her legs falling wider for me. I let the head of my dick slide between her wet folds, teasing her, making sure she's ready for me. Looking down at her beautiful face, I'm in awe that of all the cottages, she ended up in mine.

"You're so beautiful, Lilly." I let my hand caress her face.

"You don't have to woo me, Luke. I'm a sure thing."

A tiny frown falls across my face. "Can I not give you compliments?"

"I don't think what this needs is compliments."

Her words sting a little. "No matter how temporary this is …" I state while rubbing my thumb across her cheek. "It doesn't mean you deserve less."

"I'm not used to compliments," she confesses.

Jesus, her ex really was a dick to her. "Maybe I need to make you get used to them."

Her cheeks flush in embarrassment.

How does she not know how special she is?

"I don't want us to confuse what this is. I think … compliments will."

I disagree, but I can see that my words are making her uncomfortable. "So, if I said … I can't wait to sink inside of you, that would be okay?"

Lilly bites her bottom lip and nods.

"So, my dirty words are acceptable?" I nudge myself against her.

"Yes." Her eyes roll back as I slowly edge inside of her.

"If I tell you your pussy feels so fucking tight around me, that would be okay?"

"Yes," she answers on a moan as I sink fully inside her.

"That I can feel how wet you are. How much you want me."

"Yes. Yes." Her fingers grip my hips as I begin to move.

"Do you want me to tell you all the ways I have envisioned fucking you?"

"God, yes."

This makes me chuckle as I angle myself deeper, making sure I'm hitting that special bundle of nerves deep inside of her. I flip us over so I'm on my back, and she's on top of me.

"Ride me, Lilly. Show me how much you want to fuck me."

She hesitates for a moment as those bright blue eyes look down at me.

"Fuck me, Lilly," I order in Italian, and that's the only reassurance she needs because in the next moment, she arches her back, angling herself against me, and begins to do exactly that— fuck me, riding me like some champion rodeo queen.

Her gorgeous tits bounce, mesmerizing me with their dance. My dick must find the right spot because she hisses and becomes wetter with each thrust inside her.

"Harder," she tells me as I increase my thrusting.

My hand moves between us, and my thumb rubs against her clit, feeding the ache between her legs. *"Yes, go on, don't stop,"* I tell her as she rubs herself against me.

"Yes. Yes. Oh God, yes." Lilly arches again as I feel her tightening around me. "More, more," she begs, and I give her what she wants until she screams. Then I flip her over, and it's my turn to be in charge.

"Yes, you feel so good." I continue to fuck her while her fingers dig into me as my thrusts become harder and faster until I just can't hang on anymore. No matter how hard I try, her pussy is just too much.

It takes a couple of moments for us to catch our breath.

"Wow." Lilly looks up at me, her bright blue eyes sparkling, and her cheeks are flushed.

I feel invincible in this moment. Leaning down, I capture her lips against mine and kiss her. Hard. She wraps her arms around me and pulls me tighter against her. My dick twitches as he thinks round two is about to start.

"Now, that's my kind of compliment." Lilly's comment makes us both laugh.

8

LILLY

"Have you slept with him yet?" Laura asks as soon as she picks up the phone.

I haven't spoken to her in a couple of days and, well, a lot has happened since that first call. Luke and I have spent the past forty-eight hours snuggled in bed and, of course, doing other things. I don't think anyone has screwed my brains out like he has. I should've messed around with an Italian earlier. The rumors are true that they are great lovers and not selfish at all. He spends way more time satisfying me than himself, so much so, I'm in a continual state of bliss.

"Lolly!"

"You're still there, so I can only assume things are going well?"

"There's a major snowstorm, it's too dangerous to leave." Even I know it's a weak excuse.

"Baloney," my sister calls me out.

"Fine." Lowering my voice, I say, "I've spent the past couple of days in bed ..." silence falls between us as Laura waits for me to finish, "... not alone." I pull the phone away from my ear as Laura screams, deafening me.

"Fate. I told you fate has her hands in this."

"Luke has his hands in it," I joke.

"Who the hell is this person? The sister I know doesn't joke about sex," Laura teases.

"So *many* orgasms." I'm giggling. I didn't think there was such a thing, but there most definitely is.

"Oh my god, Lil. You seem like your old self. I haven't seen her in years." My sister's words catch me off-guard.

Had being with Rob really changed me that much?

"Really?"

"Yeah. You seem carefree. I mean, the old sister I knew wouldn't be hooking up with some hottie stranger. She'd have hightailed it out of there so fast. I know you would've stayed in a hotel in the village."

"I wasn't that wound up, was I?"

Laura's voice softens. "Not in a bad way ..." Which translates to 'hell yeah, you were wound up like a spring.' "Now that I know what you were going through over here, I get it." Tears begin to well in my eyes. "You hid so much about what was happening with Rob that I think it came out as being tightly wound."

Shit, she's right.

"I'm sorry."

"Babe, you have nothing to be sorry about. I'm the one who's sorry, I had no idea what was going on. I could've helped. I could have kicked his ass earlier or sent mercenaries in to kidnap you and bring you home."

"I should've told you what was going on. I just ..." The tears fall. "I knew you would try and save me."

"Only because I love you," my sister adds.

"I know. I just felt like you're always the one looking out for me. This time I wanted to work it out myself and in my own way." Silent understanding falls between us for a couple of moments.

"Enough about pin-dick Rob. I need more about the Italian Stallion."

"It's just some fun."

"And?" she pushes.

"There's an expiration date. One month. That's all."

"What happens if you fall in love with him?"

"What? No. No one falls in love after a month."

"I did with my Andy," she reminds me.

"That's because you guys are soulmates."

"Don't you think you and the Italian could be soulmates? I mean, it's a pretty awesome story to tell your kids."

"Laura," I groan her name. My sister believes in fairy tales and unicorns, but the real world isn't like that.

"Fine." I know she is rolling her eyes at me. "Just don't close yourself off."

"I need to work on me. That's my main focus."

"Okay, fine, I can handle that. Send us a picture of him. I want to see the stallion."

"I can't just snap a picture of him."

"Yes, you can ... a sneaky selfie. Tell him I need to have it as security in case something happens to you, so I know who to blame."

"Lolly, you sound like me."

"Oh, how the tables have turned." She laughs.

"So ... what have you guys been up to?" I change the subject.

"Lilly, this place is magical. When the sun sets over the national park, the golds and reds are incredible. Then you see an elephant walk past or a giraffe, and I think I'm dreaming." I chuckle at her experiences. It's the same awe she's expressing that I felt arriving in that faraway place. It was completely magical. The landscape has this unbelievable light that hits it just right, and everywhere you look, it's like you're in the middle of a

National Geographic magazine. Each time I went on safari, David Attenborough's voice echoed in my head.

"Now, see that gazelle striding through the open spaces ...? What she doesn't know is danger lurks just under the surface."

"We went to the Maasai Mara village, too. The colors, the people, they are all so beautiful." I can tell Laura has fallen in love with the country as much as I did.

"How's Andy doing?" The poor guy, he's lived a sheltered life in Glencoe, and going down to London is as overseas as he gets.

"He's blown away. I don't think he ever dreamed there were such things outside of his village. Like, he was happy there, but now? Now he is like ... I want to see more. Let's do this. Let's do that. He's turned into some kind of adventurer."

My heart fills with happiness. Even though we aren't together, I'm glad that they are experiencing the world.

"I'm so happy that something good has come out of our miscommunication."

She giggles. "Speaking of miscommunication, have you heard from pin dick?"

"Yes, I received a very pathetic email."

"What a turd face. What did it say? Read it to me."

I open my laptop and pull up my emails.

"Dearest Lilly, it starts."

"Seriously, after all those years, that's how he starts an email? Like you're some kind of stranger or his nan. This isn't the nineteenth century, ye bastard," Laura's a little fired up.

"Anyway ..." I continue.

"I'm grieved to find out that you left Africa without telling me. I thought as your fiancé you should've discussed this before one leaves."

"This man is a total douche. What? You need his permission to go away? Hell, no. You dodged a bullet there, sister."

I continue, *"I was very upset to hear from your sister the reasons why you had left. This is in no way my fault, especially with your lack of communication. How would I know that you were upset? You understand that a man has needs, and if his future wife isn't performing them, he has a right to seek help elsewhere."*

"What the actual fuck," Laura screams down the phone. "No. He didn't just say that, did he? Does he have some sort of serious stupidity disease? He has to have."

"I'm afraid he's serious. It gets worse."

"I believe that living away in the African desert can be quite trying for a woman, and so I'll give you time back home to recuperate before I expect you back by my side. I do not want to have to tell our parents about this oversight in our relationship. They will both be so displeased."

"Lilly, I don't think I hit him hard enough because this isn't right. How dare he speak to you like that."

"I know. I ignored it because I was so busy ... we worked different shifts at the hospital, and we didn't live together, so we only saw each other for dates, and they were infrequent due to being on call. So, I never saw this side of him."

"Seriously, babe, he thinks he's some Lord from the eighteenth century. His values are so archaic."

"I'm realizing now what my life would've been like if we had married."

"You know Mom and Dad are going to be displeased because nothing we do pleases them, anyway. So really, that's not a true threat, is it?" Laura states.

"Exactly, and honestly, Luke has opened my eyes to how I should've been treated. That I deserve to be happy in my work and my love life."

"Preach it, sister. Good sex will do that every time. My Andy is amazing, the things that farmer boy can do to me. It's like he's been repressed all his life and then boom, I've brought out his inner sex god."

"La, la, la, la … I don't need to know any of this." My stomach is turning as the crazy visuals hurtle through my mind.

"Fine. Just know your sister is very satisfied by a man who many would see as a boring farmer."

"Hey, I'm not boring," I hear Andy call out in the background.

"You most certainly are not." Laura giggles flirtatiously.

"Okay, I'm going to go because this has turned weird. Have fun and enjoy the sights."

"We will. Relish in your hot Italian Stallion, and remember, I want pictures."

I roll my eyes. "Love you, Lolly."

"Love you, Lilly."

I place the phone down on my bed, and a tiny tear falls down my cheek. I miss her so much, but I'm glad she's having fun because she deserves it. I close my laptop and try to forget about Rob's letter. I'm so thankful he cheated on me. Otherwise, I'd have been blind to his true personality.

Would he have made me stop practicing medicine to have children?

Would he have cheated throughout our entire marriage?

Would I be some glorified stay-at-home mother who had to make sure his dinner was on the table when he came home?

That's not at all what I want from my life. Yes, I want kids, but I also still want to practice medicine even if it's part-time. Why can't I do both?

9

LUCA

"I'm so sorry, but it's tradition," Lilly apologizes for the hundredth time.

"It's just dinner at a pub. How bad could it be?"

Her eyes widen. Is that fear I see behind those blue eyes?

"It will be an experience." She gives me a wary smile.

We're currently standing in the snow out in front of the village pub. It's Christmas Eve, and apparently, it's a tradition in the village to all come down to have dinner at the pub. There should be about a hundred people there tonight, but standing in front of the small building, I don't understand how that many people can fit inside.

"Stick close to me. Don't answer any questions you don't feel comfortable with. Tell them to keep their noses to themselves, or even better, pretend you don't speak English."

"Why would they be giving me their noses?" What an odd term.

She laughs. "No, they don't give you their noses. Just saying that they'll try and stick their noses into your business. They want all the gossip."

Right. I understand. Little does Lilly know that I have dealt with people like that all my life. I know how to handle gossips.

"Are you ready?"

It sounds like we're about to blast off on a mission to Mars with the serious tone in her voice. But she grew up here, so I guess she knows what we're in for, so I brace myself.

Lilly pushes the large wooden door open, and the once-noisy pub falls silent—all heads turn and stare at the intrusion.

"Is that Lilly Simpson?" A big, balding man makes his way over from the bar.

"It's the one and only." She smiles at him, then gives him a big hug. He picks her up off her feet and swings her around. Lilly's laughing, her giggles filling the old pub.

"Yer back from saving the world." The man's accent is so thick it's making it hard to translate.

"I am, I am. Missed you all too much." The room erupts into laughter at Lilly's joke. I can see she is well-loved by the village.

"And who's the young Jimmy wit ye," the old man asks.

"My name is Luke, not Jimmy." I hold my hand out to the old man, who just stares at it for a couple of moments before taking it in his meaty paw and shaking it to death. He bursts out laughing, a deep belly laugh, and the whole room erupts in unison. I think the joke has been lost in translation because I don't get it.

"Jimmy is the Scottish word for man," Lilly translates for me.

Oh, I see, and I give the old man a smile.

"I'm Wallace, ah ain this pub."

Okay, that can't have been English, so I look to Lilly for help.

"Wallace owns the pub," Lilly says, translating.

The old man is puffing out his chest while slowly breaking my hand.

"It's nice," I tell him, looking around at the establishment.

It's not really where you would find me normally, but it has a kind of rural charm about it. The dark wooden beams, the stone floor that's covered in old, well-worn rugs, and there are leather bar stools around the bar. Old photographs of Scottish towns line the tartan wallpapered walls. An old stag head sits proudly on one wall, and a stone fireplace sits across another. There's a scattering of leather booths filled with people, candles flickering in the middle, giving it a rugged kind of ambiance. There are more wooden tables scattered around, all set for dinner, with people of various ages dining, and they're staring right at me. Some with curiosity, some with indifference, and even some with disdain. I'm guessing they aren't fond of outsiders.

"Luke's Contessa's nephew." Lilly sticks with the same lie she told the other day.

"Och, Contessa," Wallace tells me. "God rest her soul." I understood those words and move my attention to the floor in respect.

"We met briefly at the funeral. Laura has asked him to come out for the holidays to look after the cottage while she and Andy went on holiday."

This all sounds pretty close to the truth.

"She went to see you. Why are you not there?" a woman pipes up from the corner.

"That's because I came home to surprise her, Seonaid," Lilly tells the woman. "And she went to Africa to surprise me ... a series of unfortunate events."

They all nod at her comments.

"But what about that young man you were dating ... the doctor?" another woman in the corner asks.

Lilly visibly stills, being put on the spot like that in front of everyone can't be easy. I place my hand on the small of her back, and Wallace eyes me suspiciously. "Unfortunately, Rob and I are no longer together." There are gasps from the captive audience. "He wasn't at all who I thought he was."

The women seem to all nod in understanding.

"Ne'er liked him anyway," replied Seonaid, who I remember Lilly telling me was the town gossip. Then she adds, "Thought he was too good for folk like us," she adds.

I hear murmurs from the people filtering through in agreement.

"Is he yer new man?" she asks.

"We're just friends."

I'm pretty sure we're not 'just friends' but they don't need to know that.

Lilly's cheeks are red from the interrogation.

"He's very cute," another lady pipes in.

"Wynda, behave," Lilly scolds the old lady with the bright blue curly hair, who winks at me.

"I wouldn't behave with him in my cottage." The women all squeal with laughter at the old lady's brazen remarks.

"Italians make good lovers," a lady from behind the bar adds.

"All right, Donna, am standin' rite 'ere," Wallace says to the woman.

"Scots make the best lovers." She blows the giant man a kiss. He rolls his eyes but winks back at her.

"Noo, c'mon, let's git ye a drink," Wallace says, and I'm lost again.

Lilly grabs my hand, and I see the gossip's eyes widen at the action as she brings me over to the bar where Donna's serving.

"Two whiskies on the rocks, please," Lilly asks.

Donna nods and starts preparing our drinks.

"I'm so sorry about that. We can go home if you want?" I can see it on Lilly's face, she'd go if I asked her to, but that's not going to happen.

"No, I'm fine. This is great. It's different to my home." I could just imagine what my father's face would be like seeing me sitting at some pub, sipping subpar whisky with people he'd deem lower class than him. "If I get stuck, I'll call out to you in Italian."

"The old ladies will probably have a heart attack at your hotness if you whip your native tongue out."

I lean in a little closer to her. *"You like it when I whip my tongue out, don't you?"* I say in Italian so no one can hear.

Lilly's jaw drops and she blinks a few times in shock. *"I can't believe you just said that, in front of all these people,"* she scolds me in perfect Italian.

It's the first time I've heard her speak my language in a complete sentence, and I like it.

"Here's ye drinks." Donna hands over two glasses of whisky to us before moving on to others waiting to be served.

"You speaking Italian is hot."

Lilly gives me the side-eye, but no one can understand what we're saying. I doubt any of them can speak Italian. *"Stop it,"* Lilly hisses.

"Fine, but tonight, I'm not going to stop. No matter how many times you ask me to."

Lilly takes an unsteady gulp of her whisky while her cheeks pink the exact color they go when I make her come.

The night continues quite nicely, much to my surprise. Everyone is lovely in the village, and it seems they very much look out for Lilly as one of their own. You can see how proud they are of her for the work she's done in Africa, and the way they affectionately talk about Lilly's nan, which made her teary a couple of times, but she assured me she was fine.

"I've missed this food." Lilly licks her lips.

We have just finished a soup called Cock-a-leekie. I thought Lilly was playing a joke on me when she told me about it, but she wasn't. What a strange name. Couldn't imagine serving that at one of our family dinners, my mother would probably have a heart attack at the sinful name. Then I watch in shock as they bring out platters of large roasted turkeys, baked vegetables, and sauces.

"Lilly." I nudge her gently. "At home ... we don't eat meat on Christmas Eve, *giorno di magro*, we eat lean to purify our body for Christmas Day."

Lilly's eyes widen.

"Oh, shit! They are going to think you don't like their food if you don't eat it. This is a huge tradition in Scotland to have a big roast turkey with all the trimmings. We can pretend there was an emergency phone call and leave. I can get takeout for us and go home and have something you would normally have."

My world stops at that moment. She's having a great time, but because I mentioned feeling a little uneasy about breaking my tradition, she didn't even second-guess it. She's willing to pack up and eat our dinner at home.

No, I can't let her do that. She's just come home from living in the bush for the last couple of years. Her sister is on the other side of the world, her parents are in London and don't seem to communicate with her, and the two people she was closest with have passed away.

"It looks delicious. I can't wait to try it all," I tell her as I dig in.

Lilly's hand reaches under the table, linking our fingers together. "Thank you."

I want to kiss her in this moment, not caring if all these people see.

She is an extraordinary woman, nothing like I've ever met before.

10

LILLY

Luke had one too many whiskies last night, I think, judging by the snoring he was doing this morning when I woke up beside him. I'm glad he had fun. I could tell it was a cultural shock for him, but he embraced it as did the village, especially the old ladies. They loved giving him hugs and squishing his cheeks, and not the ones on his face. Poor guy was totally manhandled by the geriatrics.

Last night, Luke told me his tradition on Christmas Eve was to eat no meat to purify your body for Christmas Day, and because he didn't get that last night, I want to do an Italian Christmas for him today, as much as I can with the limited food I have left in the pantry. I've spent the morning googling menus from the regions he said he lives in, and I think I have some items to make him something that might resemble Italian food with a bit of Scottish thrown in for good measure.

"Morning." Luke groggily enters the kitchen.

"Merry Christmas." I call out to him.

Luke stills, rubs his eyes, hungover and stares at me. "It's Christmas?"

"Yes."

He slumps down onto the armchair beside the fire, his voice is a little rough from all his singing last night.

"Huh." He stares at the crackling fire for a long couple of moments.

Maybe Luke isn't that much of a morning person.

Then, he suddenly jumps up and rushes toward me, grabbing my face and kissing me.

"Buon Natale, *Merry Christmas,*" he says. "Sorry, that's what I should've done when I first walked in," he states as he leans back against the island.

"You had a wild night," I respond, turning back to my pots that are bubbling away on the stove.

"Those old people can drink." He shakes his head.

"Never get in a drinking contest with a Scotsman. You'll always lose."

"Now, I know." He chuckles. "What are you doing?" he asks, noticing the pots.

"I'm attempting to make an Italian Christmas."

His mouth opens in shock. "What?"

"Last night you experienced a Scottish Christmas. So, I think to be fair, now you get to have an Italian one."

He grabs me again and kisses my face all over. "Of all the cottages you walked into, I'm glad it was mine."

"Technically, you walked into mine." I elbow him.

"You're always so analytical," he jokes, then he starts tickling me.

"Stop it. Stop it." My stomach is hurting from all the giggling because I'm so ticklish.

Luke pulls me back into his arms again. "I'm very happy that you came home when you did. There isn't anyone else in the world I'd want to spend Christmas with today." Luke's words set butterflies off in my belly.

"Well, I hope you still feel that way after lunch. I can't guarantee the food will be totally authentic."

Luke kisses me gently again. "It smells delicious. Let me go have a shower, then I can help you."

It's only been a couple of days since being home, but it feels like a lifetime.

How have I become so close to a stranger in such a short time?

Is it because we're forced together?

Is it chemistry?

Is it because all we have is time to get to know each other without outside interference?

Does it really matter why?

It's not like you're going to marry the guy. He's a holiday romance. Once his time is up, that's it, he'll be a lovely memory.

I hear a raised voice coming from down the hallway. Who is Luke arguing with? He's talking in rapid Italian, and I can't quite catch what he's saying. *You shouldn't be listening, Lilly.* He has a right to have a private conversation. A short time later, Luke storms into the kitchen looking agitated, swearing under his breath.

"Are you okay?"

He stills, looking at me, his face softening. "Just business stuff."

"On Christmas Day?" Who calls their boss on Christmas Day? An asshole, that's who.

"My business is kind of twenty-four-seven," he adds quickly.

I haven't pushed him about what he does for a living. I haven't really pushed him much about his life as he doesn't seem to want to talk about it.

He then pulls me into his arms and kisses me gently. "When I'm around you, you make me feel calm. That nothing outside this cottage exists."

I know what he means.

Grabbing my ass and lifting me on top of the kitchen counter, he pushes open my legs. Thankfully, I'm still in my sleep shirt and knee-high socks. *My toes get cold.* He easily fits between my legs, which I wrap around his thick waist.

"Is anything going to burn if I take your attention away for at least ten minutes? I can make it quick, just this once." He smirks at me.

I look over his shoulder and check what I'm cooking. Yeah, it should be fine. I mean, if anything starts to burn, I'm just here.

"Should be okay."

He pushes up the hem of my sleep shirt, exposing my underwear.

"Good." He rips my underwear off in one easy tug. Holy shit! He just ripped my underwear off. That's some kind of porn star move. I mean, damn, those knickers were flimsy AF. I thought Marks & Spencer was supposed to have good-quality underwear. They shouldn't tear like that. Wish I had my receipt, I could've taken them back for faulty workmanship.

"Lilly."

I pause my inner monologue and look up at him.

"You were in your head again." *I was.* "Let me help you focus on other things." He pulls me to the edge of the island, giving me a devious grin, before opening my legs. Thick thumbs tease my outer folds, back and forth, until they slowly slip in.

My hands hit the counter. My head falls back as the electricity begins to pump through my veins. He continues until his fingers are slick with my arousal.

When I open my eyes, I notice his track pants are down around his ankles, and he's sheathing himself. "Sorry, it's a quickie this morning, but I need you."

My teeth sink into my bottom lip at his confession.

He needs me. Yeah, that has to be like lighting a barrel of gunpowder at a woman's vagina. That comment makes a woman combust in mere seconds. *He needs me.* They are three words all women want to hear.

Luke pushes himself inside me, and I love the feeling of

stretching all around him. We're connecting at this moment as close as any two people can be. Those chocolate eyes are intense as he fills me. He doesn't move. We just share the moment of raw togetherness.

His forehead falls to my shoulder. "You were an unexpected surprise, Lilly." I could say the same thing about him. "And most of the time, I don't know what to do with you." This isn't the sexy times I thought we'd be having. "You've opened my mind to many new things that I never dared possible."

My dirty-talking Luke has been replaced by a philosophical Luke.

"I ..." Luke pulls himself nearly out of me, his fingers gripping into the flesh of my ass, then drives himself back into me, pushing me hard against the countertop. "I never thought ..." He pushes inside of me again, deeper, seeking to be as connected as we can be. "I never thought there could be another way." My mind is swirling with orgasmic fog. What's he talking about? "You're special, Lil."

His perfect rhythm is taking over as he continuously slams himself into me. Now, that's my version of what a quickie is all about. We both hurtle toward each other's orgasms, higher and higher until we reach that peak simultaneously, then slump against each other, heaving with strenuous exertion.

"That was ... different."

Luke looks up at me with a frown on his face.

"Your dirty talking was a little different than what you normally say."

"I'm sorry about that," he quickly adds, looking slightly uncomfortable for the first time, ever.

"Hey." Pulling his face to mine, not letting him feel embarrassed about sharing a part of himself with me, I say, "I didn't say I didn't like it." Pressing a kiss against the stubble of the beard he's starting to grow, I continue, "I was just wondering where it came from."

He's shutting down on me. The fog of his orgasm has gone.

"Let me clean up first." He pulls himself out of me and walks toward the bathroom. I have no panties anymore, so there's no point putting them on. I'd better disinfect the countertop too. I grab the spray and quickly wipe it down before following after Luke.

"Hey ... don't shut down on me, it's Christmas." Yep, pulling out the 'it's Christmas' guilt card.

Luke lets out a sigh and turns around. "I'm sorry, Lilly. The phone call was from my family. They want me to come home."

My stomach drops. "Oh."

"Like you, I kind of left in a hurry."

I know that feeling, so I get it.

"Honestly, it's too soon to go back. I need more time away, especially from them, they are very controlling."

I nod in understanding. My parents are the same, hence why I didn't hightail it back to London and chose Glencoe instead.

"I want more time with you." He grabs my hand and kisses the delicate skin of my wrist. "The more time I spend with you, Lilly, the more I find myself."

Boom.

There go the butterflies in my stomach. The cage that's been holding them in just exploded, and I can feel them flittering around.

"Oh ..." Yeah, that's a brilliant answer when a man tells you that you make him a better person.

"I'm moving too fast ..." Luke takes a step away from me, running his hands through his silky, black hair. "Forget what I said ..." He pushes past me and heads to the front door where our boots and jackets are located.

"Hey," I call out after him.

He slowly turns around, and I can see the tiniest bit of hurt across his face.

I run to him and jump into his arms, nearly barreling him

over. I place a sloppy wet kiss on his face, which makes him laugh.

"You're crazy, Lil." He chuckles.

"Yeah, about you." The words slip out too easily, and he stills.

"Yeah?" The cocky smirk crosses his face.

"Yeah." My arms wrap around his neck. "I think you're a bit of all right."

He raises an eyebrow at me, which makes my eyes roll.

"Now ... enough feelings for the moment. Let's get cooking, so you can work these calories I'm about to eat off me."

Luke's palms squeeze my ass. "I like the sound of that."

11

LILLY

Okay, when I said he was going to help me work off my Christmas lunch calories, I thought it was going to be by the fire or in our bed, not walking through the damn snow. I cooked a brilliant Christmas lunch, not traditional at all, but it was still delicious. I made spaghetti carbonara even though Luke burned the bacon.

Like, seriously, how do you burn bacon?

Well, now I understand how one burns bacon when they have never cooked before.

I think Luke might be a mommy's boy. He is Italian, and their moms are notorious for looking after their sons. But we survived. I also made bruschetta to start which Luke complimented me on, and I even attempted tiramisu—with the awful instant coffee—

which didn't turn out too bad. Luke ate it all so that's a win. He was pleased I had gone to the effort to make him feel at home today. I haven't really celebrated Christmas the past two years—sick people don't usually stop for us to celebrate.

"Hurry up," Luke calls ahead of me.

"My legs are little, and the snow is deep," I call back. I don't have stilts for legs like him. In some places I sink down all the way to my bum. I'm not made for this. Luke makes his way back to me, picks me up, and hauls me over his shoulder like a fireman.

"What are you doing?" I squeal.

"It will be quicker if I just carry you," he tells me as he makes quick work through the snow. He's right, he's walking quicker without me straggling behind him.

We don't get far until I start complaining about being ill—hanging upside down isn't a great idea after a big meal.

"Jump onto my back." He crouches, and I jump on—now that's better.

"Giddy up." I pretend Luke's a horse and slap his bum, he's not that amused, but I'm having fun.

We eventually make it down to the lake called Loch Leven, which is a famous lake in the area. Some of it is frozen over, while some of it still has running water. There isn't a person out, we're the only crazy people out in the cold like this. But it's peaceful, relaxing, soothing, and great for the constitution.

"This is beautiful." Luke looks out at the white landscape. "Peaceful." Both of us take in the majesty of the mountains, snow, and lake. "Do you think Rob will want you back?" Luke's question surprises me—it's come out of nowhere—and I draw my brows together.

"He can try, but as far as I'm concerned, we're through. I wasn't in love with him. I think …" I hesitate, kicking the snow in front of me. "I think I dated him to get my parents' approval." There it is—the truth.

Can I really fault Rob for cheating on me when I was never really in the relationship? That I was never in love with him?

Luke is silent as if he's contemplating something.

"I understand that. My business … it's the family business, and I have a lot of responsibility on my shoulders." He's finally opening up about himself.

"Are you the oldest?"

"No, thankfully. So, I have a tiny bit of freedom compared to my brother, but I'm next in line."

"How many in your family?"

"I have an older brother and two younger sisters."

"Are you close with them?" I don't want to ask too many questions and spook him, but I like him telling me more about himself.

"With my brother and youngest sister, yes, but the other sister ..." He shakes his head. "She ... she's best friends with my ex."

His ex? I knew he could possibly have one, but it still shocks me to hear him say it out loud. "She chose sides?" I ask.

He huffs. "Very much so. From her text messages, she is very much on Team Rachele." Luke kicks some snow in front of him. "She cheated on me ..."

My stomach sinks. Who the hell would be stupid enough to cheat on this man?

"With my best friend."

"What? No."

"Yep." He shoves his hands into his pockets.

"That's the worst kind of disloyalty because they both betrayed you." He nods. "Why?" I don't understand why people cheat with best friends.

"I don't know. I didn't stay around long enough to find out."

Guess we're more alike than I thought.

"Did you love her?"

Luke contemplates that question for a couple of moments. "I thought what we had was love, but I realize now that it was just what was expected of us ... to be together. I guess like you, our families are friends and had been for a very long time, and everyone just assumed we'd one day get married." I know exactly what he means. "I had to get away, and I'm glad I have. It's given me a new perspective on my life." Luke holds out his hand to me, I take it, my cheeks warming at the simple gesture.

We both sit together on a rock in silence, at one with nature.

After a short time, my body starts to shiver, so I declare, "I'm so cold." I'm trembling all over when we finally make it back into the warmth of the cottage.

"Let me run you a bath." That sounds like a fantastic idea.

As I slowly take off my frozen outer clothing, then hang it on the clothes rack near the door, I hear my phone ringing in my room and make a mad dash to it as I haven't heard from Laura yet.

"Hello," I answer, grabbing it before it rings out.

"Merry Christmas, Lilly," Laura and Andy shout. Hearing their voices today makes the holiday feel right.

"Merry Christmas, guys. Where are you?"

"We're in Zanzibar." Laura squeals.

Oh, wow!

"It's beautiful there … very romantic."

"I know …" there's a pause, then she continues, "… it totally was because Andy proposed," she screams down the phone.

"No way." I squeal back.

"Yep, yep, yep … I'm going to be a bride." I can feel Laura's enthusiasm, and it warms my heart.

"Oh my god, guys, I'm so happy for you." Tears are falling down my cheeks because I miss my sister and wish I could give her a big hug to celebrate this momentous occasion with her.

The line crackles. "We better go. The line isn't too good," she says, now fading in and out.

"Love you."

The phone goes dead, and I'm not sure if she heard the last part. I sit on the bed, tears rolling down my cheeks.

"Lilly, are you okay? What happened?" Luke asks, wrapping his arms around me, not realizing it's exactly what I need at this moment as I cry into his chest.

"My sister is getting married." I sniffle.

"That's good ... no?" he asks, confused by my reaction.

"It's good. So good. I'm happy ..." I burst into tears again.

Yeah, poor Luke is most definitely out of his depth at the moment.

"Come, come ... a hot bath will do you good." He picks me up in his arms and walks with me to the bathroom.

I like the way he just picks me up as if I weigh as much as a feather. It's so manly being shifted around like this. He slowly undresses me, not in a sexual way, but in a caring way. He too undresses, and we both ease into the hot water, my extremities burning at the heat until I sink in and lay back against Luke's chest. He runs his fingers through my hair, soothing me.

"I'm so happy for her ..." I start, holding in my emotions. "I just wish I was there to celebrate it with her." I close my eyes as Luke massages my head.

"I understand you want to celebrate with them. But they are in Africa, a very romantic place. It's nice that they have this moment between the two of them."

He's right.

I'm being selfish.

They need this time together.

I can celebrate with them both when they get back. I don't have to do it seconds after she announces her news.

I sink deeper into the water. "You're a wise one, Mr. Luke."

I hear him chuckle beside my ear. "That would be a first."

We lay in the warm water and talk. Luke tells me all about his travels abroad, and I tell him about the exciting things I did while in Kenya, funnily enough, most of the time without Rob. He wasn't interested in the culture of the country unless there were diplomats or ambassadors coming to visit, and we were being invited to VIP dinners. Working in Africa was a once-in-a-lifetime achievement, something I'd never trade in a million years.

Maybe fate does have a hand in things.

Oh, no, is Laura's influence sinking in? Am I seriously contemplating fate?

Maybe that's why Luke was brought into my life, to pull me in another direction, to show me there are other options.

Perhaps there's something to be said about fate.

12

LUCA

After our bath, I took Lilly to my bed where I showed her how much I appreciated the Italian Christmas she put together for me. I showed her repeatedly. She's currently snoring softly beside me, her light brown hair spread out all around her. The sheet has fallen, exposing her breast, and all I want to do is suck on that nipple, but that would wake her, and she's exhausted after our hike earlier in the day.

I didn't mean to tell her about Rachele because if she googles our names, my cover will be blown and, in all honesty, I know things will change between us once she knows who I am.

My phone rings, and I pick it up. "Ciao," I answer without looking to see who it is.

"Lilly?" the male voice says down the line.

Oh shit! This is Lilly's phone which I picked up by accident. Looking down at the screen, I see the word 'Rob' staring back at me. Fuck.

"Lilly? Hello, is this Lilly's phone?"

Dammit! What do I do?

I don't think she wants Rob to know about me, especially because of the family drama she has told me about.

"Lilly, are you there? Are you okay?"

I do the only thing that's right and hang up on him. Moments later, her phone rings, and it's him again, so I hang up on him, but he calls again and again and again.

"Luke?" Lilly opens her eyes and looks up at me. "What's going on?"

My stomach sinks. "I accidentally answered your phone."

Her face turns a little pale when it starts ringing again, and she sees whose name it is on the other end.

"I didn't say anything other than Ciao. I thought it was my phone. Sorry, I was half asleep." She grabs the phone angrily out of my hand and sits up in bed.

"What do you want, Rob?" she answers, anger lacing her voice.

"Who the hell answered your phone?" I hear Rob scream down the line at her.

"No one."

Why does her calling me no one sting?

"I heard a male's voice, Lilly."

She rolls her eyes at his question. "So."

"So?" he screams at her. "My fiancée shouldn't be entertaining other men."

"Really? And when was the last time you fucked someone else?" Lilly asks Rob. The line suspiciously goes quiet for a couple of moments. "That's what I thought."

"You left me," he screams at her. "You walked out on me. What was I supposed to do?"

Is this guy serious? What a fucking dick.

Lilly closes her eyes and bangs her head against the headboard in frustration, then answers, "Anything you want, Rob. I don't care who you screw around with, just like you shouldn't care who I'm screwing around with." She sounds eerily calm, she is done with him.

"So, you're screwing him? I knew it. I knew you were a

fucking slut. A worthless fucking lay. It won't take him long till he's fucking someone else because you're fucking shit."

I see the moment Lilly shuts down over his words. That each one of his barbs hits her right in the heart, and he fucking knows it. Asshole.

I see red.

Reaching over, I rip the phone from her.

"Now, listen here, you little piece of shit. Just because a pin dick like you couldn't keep a woman like Lilly satisfied doesn't mean anyone else can't. She's the most amazing woman I have ever met, and the fact that you have no idea the fucking gem you had right in front of you means one man's loss is another man's gain. I can tell you something ... there's no way I'll ever want to fuck another woman because there is no one on this earth who's like Lilly Simpson." With that, I hang up the phone and throw it across the room. I still, realizing what I've just done. "Oh shit, Lil. I'm so sorry, I ..."

The next thing I know, Lilly's jumping into my arms and kissing me. Thankfully, we're both still naked.

"Thank you," she tells me through kisses.

We fall back against the bed, me on top of her. She wraps her legs around my hips and pulls me closer, my dick nudging at her entrance—my unsheathed dick. I've never wanted to fuck someone bare more than Lilly in this moment, but I can't.

Breaking our kiss, I lean over and grab a condom.

"Let me just ..." I fiddle with the latex, and once I'm sheathed, I enter her, and then everything feels right in the world.

13

LILLY

I'm awakened by Luke entering me, and it feels so fucking good. Arching my back as his hands palm my breasts, I don't think I'll ever get sick of sleeping with this man. He takes his time this morning, slow and steady, a little less frantic than our session last night. I can't believe he came to my rescue like that. It's going to cause a shitstorm of problems for me once Rob runs off to my parents and tattles on me, but right here, right now, I don't care. Maybe it's the bubble of the cottage that's made me throw caution to the wind, but no one is going to ruin this good mood I'm in.

It doesn't take us long until we both find our release.

"Morning ..." Luke nuzzles my neck.

"Good morning to you, too."

"I like being able to have you when I want," he whispers against my neck, his warm breath sending shivers all over my body.

"I like it, too."

"Come ... let's grab a shower. I then want another round of Monopoly because this time, I'm going to kick your ass." The bed dips as Luke slides out of it.

"Oh, someone's feeling cocky this morning." Turning around and looking at a very naked Luke before me, my eyes dip to his impressive dick that's still hard after our morning session.

"You just can't seem to keep your eyes off my cock. So yes, I'm feeling awfully cocky."

My mouth falls open in surprise before bursting out laughing.

"It's not my fault you keep boosting my ego."

Picking up the pillow, I throw it at him in a fit of laughter. He, of course, catches it easily and throws it to the floor, stalks toward me, and pulls me from the bed. I have the sheet wrapped around me as he hauls me over his shoulder again.

It's so primal the way he does that.

Is it an Italian thing?

I've never had a guy throw me around so much.

He places me gently down on the bathroom floor, then slaps my ass. "Get in the shower, Lilly."

We have another session in the shower because, hello, running your hands all over that spectacular body it's way too hard not to get turned on. Honestly, I have never had so much sex in my life. Italian men are incredibly giving. I get the nickname Italian Stallion now because Luke's stamina is phenomenal.

We finally emerge and set up a game of Monopoly.

"You're going down," Luke tells me as we begin the game.

"Oh yeah, I am …" I wiggle my eyebrows at him.

"Don't you try and distract me with your feminine wiles. I'm not going to fall for it."

"I think I remember you were the one who distracted me last time." I smile over at him.

"I didn't see you complaining about it." That cocky smirk he gives me gets me every single time.

We've now been playing the game for an hour or so, one very heated hour as the competitiveness between both of us takes over.

"No, I'm not going to do a deal with you. Then you would have a set." Luke moans.

Not my fault I'm awesome at this game.

"Look, I can give you ..." Looking at my cards, I try to find something that might sweeten the pot, but then there's a loud banging at the door. We both freeze while the banging continues.

"Stay here," Luke tells me protectively as he rushes over to answer the door.

Cold air rushes inside as soon as the door is open.

"Lilly. We need Lilly. There's been an accident." I can hear a man's voice calling out.

Jumping out of my chair, I rush to the front door and see Alfie Stewart, Andy's youngest brother.

"Alfie, what's going on?" Worry courses through my veins. Has something happened to Laura and Andy in Africa?

"Nan's had a fall. There is lots of blood." His face turns pale at his words.

"Is she conscious?" He nods his head. "Okay, let me grab my stuff. I'll meet you there," I tell Alfie before rushing around the cottage finding my boots and a jacket.

"I'll come with you," Luke adds, grabbing his jacket.

I look up at him. "You don't have to."

"I can drive," he adds.

"Fine. Let me grab the first-aid kit, and let's go."

We head out in the snowstorm and carefully make our way over to the Stewart's farm. I can see smoke billowing out of their chimney, the bright glow of the lights on at Nanny Stewart's cottage. Grabbing my kit from out the back of Luke's 4WD, I head on down the snowy path and open the wooden doors.

"Lilly." Margaret, Andy's mom, wraps her arms around me. "Thank you so much for coming in this weather. Doc Finnigan is on holiday." Her eyes widen over my shoulder as Luke walks in behind me. "Oh my ..." I can see her taking in Luke's form behind me.

Glencoe isn't used to seeing someone as exotic as Luke around these parts.

I stomp my feet a couple of times, shaking off the snow from my boots, the sound bringing Margaret back to the present. Quickly, I shuck them off and follow her to where Nanny Stewart is currently sitting on the kitchen chair. There's a nasty gash on her forehead, and blood dripping down all over her nightgown. Bernard, Andy's dad, is cleaning up the bloody mess on the kitchen floor.

"Lilly Simpson," Nanny Stewart calls out. *That's good she's still coherent.* "I told them not to fuss." She looks around at her family. The woman is almost ninety, but age doesn't stop her from being independent.

"I know, but I think it's better to be safe, don't you think?" I say, walking over to her.

"Oh my … I must be concussed because I see the handsomest man I've ever seen in my almost ninety years …" she smiles, "… and I've seen many."

Her attention is being pulled to where Luke stands in the doorway—naughty little thing.

"This is Luke. He's a guest at the cottage."

"Buona serata, signora Stewart. *Have a good evening,"* he says to her, turning on all his Italian charm. I think I heard all the females in a radius of one hundred yards collectively sigh.

"Oh … he's Italian." Nanny Stewart fans her face. "You know they say Italians are the best lovers," she whispers that last bit to me making me laugh as I begin to clean up her wound.

"Ma," Bernard chastises his mother, but I can see a smirk on his face.

Nanny Stewart waves him off. "He's a vast improvement from that horrible Englishman she was dating."

"Nanny Stewart!" Now, it's Alfie's turn to tell Nan off, and I laugh.

"You know, I'm English, too."

Nanny Stewart simply shakes her head. "We consider you one of us Scots. You've spent more time up here than down *there*," she says with a little disdain for London.

Even after a couple of millennia, the rivalry between England and Scotland is still very much alive.

"It looks like I'm going to have to give you some stitches, Nanny Stewart. I promise they won't hurt at all."

"Sweetheart, I gave birth to that boofhead over there with no drugs, and he was a nine-pounder."

"Ma," Bernard moans with a smile.

"Why do you think I only had one child. If they had vagina tightening back in my day, maybe I'd have had more." The room erupts into hollers at Nanny Stewart's use of the word 'vagina.'

Turning my head to check on Luke, I see him leaning against the wall with his arms crossed and a big grin on his face.

I use numbing cream around the wound.

"Sweetheart," Nanny Stewart calls out to Luke. "Would you mind holding my hand?" She holds out her thin hand to him.

"I'd be honored, signora." Giving her his megawatt smile, he takes her hand and gently kisses it.

"Such a gentleman." She swoons. "Lilly, did you see that?"

"Yes, I did." I smile at her as I prepare everything for the stitches.

"You know our Lilly is single and a very successful doctor," she tells Luke.

"Si, I have heard."

"She's a catch."

"I can tell," he adds.

"She'd be different from the normal women you have dated." Those shrewd eyes glare at him, and Luke seems surprised at her comment.

"Ma, stop matchmaking." Margaret groans.

"Laura's almost married off. Why can't we marry off Lilly,

too?" Nanny Stewart seems a little surprised that this hasn't been done yet.

"I'm sorry, Lilly," Margaret apologizes.

"Signora," Luke addresses her. "Lilly and I have both just finished complicated relationships." Nanny Stewart's eyes go wide at his honesty. "It's not our time yet."

He said yet?

Wait! What? Concentrate on what you're doing, Lilly.

Nanny Stewart's eyes narrow as she takes in Luke's words. "I think that's fair, I like your honesty, young man." Wow. That *is* high praise coming from her. "Don't let those glossy models distract you from something genuine," she advises him.

Luke gives her a large smile. "I'm starting to see what you mean, signora."

Laugh lines appear around Nanny Stewart's eyes as she smiles so widely.

"All done," I state, finishing up my handiwork. "And it won't even leave a scar," I let her know while packing up my stuff. "Someone should stay with her overnight, though. Keep an eye on her because she doesn't seem like she's suffering from any concussion ..." especially with her shrewd line of questioning, "... but we can never be too careful."

"Thank you so much, Lilly," Margaret says.

The Stewart family all hug me—this is the family I wish I had. They're warm, loving, and supportive.

"It was a pleasure to meet you, Signora Stewart." Luke bends down and kisses her on the cheek.

"Careful, boy, we don't want Nanny to have a heart attack." Bernard bursts out laughing after he says it.

Luke stills for a moment then realizes it's a joke.

Margaret pulls me off to one side. "Laura filled me in on what's happened with Rob. Are you okay?"

"Yeah, I think I am. He wasn't the one for me."

"You deserve better, sweetheart. Just remember that."

Margaret gives me a warm, motherly hug, and I let her, sinking into her softness.

My eyes well, but I shake off my emotions.

"Are you okay staying in the cottage with this gorgeous stranger?" she questions me.

"Yeah, he's a good guy."

"Handsome, too." Margaret eyes me suspiciously.

"Yes, he is."

"Well, I hope you have fun." She winks at me.

How does she know? "It's only for a month," I tell her.

"Sometimes when you least expect it, fate has other plans."

She's been speaking to Laura.

"You ready?" Luke places his hand on the small of my back. Margaret hugs him farewell while her husband rolls his eyes with a grin.

"Now, call us if you need anything," Margaret calls out to us as we make our way back to the car. Luke opens my door, then walks around to his side. Margaret gives me a thumbs-up when she sees that gesture, and I simply shake my head and laugh.

"They are lovely," Luke tells me as he puts the 4WD into gear and heads back up the snowy highway to our cottage.

"They are good people."

"Not many people seem to like your ex?" he questions.

"I know. I always thought it was because he was English. Now I realize it's because he was a dick."

Luke chuckles at my statement.

"You seem to have won over the women … being all Italian." I wave my hands around at him.

"What does that mean?"

"Oh, don't you play coy with me. You amped up all your sexy Italian-ness for them."

"Don't know what you're talking about." He grins, keeping his eyes on the road.

"Yes, you do." Slapping his thigh with my hand, I then put on a fake manly Italian accent and pretend to be him.

"I don't sound like that." He rolls his eyes at me, but his smirk is firmly in place.

"You know exactly what you do to women. I bet you use it to your advantage in business as well by charming the pants off them."

He shakes his head. "I never sleep with a client."

"Doesn't mean you don't charm them in other ways," I tease him.

"It worked on you." Luke looks over at me, and there's heat behind his chocolate eyes.

"I seem to recall that I was the one who made the first move," I remind him.

"Seems that you, too, are equally as charming."

His words make me smile.

14

LILLY

As soon as we walk back into the cottage and into our bubble again, we are ripping off our clothes. Honestly, I have never wanted to sleep with someone as much as I want to with Luke. I mean, the man's a sexy Roman god, and any woman would be jumping him every chance they got. When he talks dirty in Italian, I'm done for.

I'm not going to let my mind run away with me this time. I don't want to be that girl trying to find a meaning behind every single compliment Luke gives me. I want to be the carefree, no-strings-attached kind of girl.

Most booty calls don't live with you.

Usually, you can separate sex and the more domestic stuff because you aren't together all the time. But when he does things like clean up after I have cooked dinner—watching him scrub the dishes has never been so erotic—yes, that's when I know I'm losing my mind. I must have cabin fever.

Rolling over, the space beside me is empty. Opening my eyes, it seems Luke is already up.

Stretching my super tired muscles, I slide out of bed and relieve myself before joining him.

"*Good morning, beautiful,*" he calls in Italian from the armchair beside the fire where he's playing on his phone. "You slept in."

My eyes widen at his comment. "Why? What time is it?" I search around with my eyes for my phone which must be still in my bedroom.

"It's 11:36."

"Wow. I never sleep in that late."

Luke reaches out and pulls me into his arms, I snuggle into his chest.

"That's because I keep you exhausted most nights." He kisses my head.

"That you do," I hum against his hard chest.

I'm going to miss this when it's all over. It's been a week. One whole week, but it feels like a lifetime. New Year's Eve is coming up, the start of a new year with so much possibility and so much expectation. My new year is going to be looking a hell of a lot different than I thought it was going to be.

One, I'm halfway across the world.

Two, I'm single.

Maybe it's a good thing.

I can now concentrate on what I want to do with my life without outside influences. I've always done what my parents wanted me to do, except going to Africa. Well, they were totally fine with it once Rob told them he thought it was an amazing idea, and that it would look good on the resume. Then, they thought it was a fabulous idea, but only because Rob agreed to it. They would've fought me all the way if he didn't want to go, and I'd have given in. My parents and Rob would have all pressured me into doing what they wanted, and because I'm so worried about disappointing everyone, I just give in. That bullshit has to stop here and now. This new year is going to be the year of Lilly, and it's going to be all about my needs and wants.

"There you go lost in your head again," he says, but I can hear the smile in his words.

I sit up in his arms, then turn and look down at him, at his gorgeous face. "Can we be friends when this is all over?" My question causes his mouth to fall open and his head to fall back in surprise. "When you have to go back to Italy."

A frown falls across Luke's face, and his body tightens. "Do you not want to sleep with me anymore?"

"Oh, God, no." Leaning down, I give him a reassuring kiss. "While you're here, I still want to sleep with you."

His shoulders loosen slightly as the tension ebbs from his body.

"But I mean, when you go back to your normal life. I don't want to be a stalker or anything, and I totally understand if you want this to be a holiday thing, and ..." I trail off because I'm rambling.

"Take a breath, Lilly." Luke finally smiles at me.

"Sorry, I ..."

"You want to be Facebook friends?" he asks.

"I guess to start with, but ..." Dammit. I'm not finding the right words here. "I just like you for you." His eyes widen. "You have a gorgeous shell, but honestly, I like talking to the man inside that shell. Hanging out ... I mean outside of the sex."

"You do?" He seems surprised, so I nod in agreement.

"Look, I don't want to cramp your style because I know you have a lot of women after you." He rolls his eyes. "You know it's true." I give him a small smile. "It's almost a new year, and I've decided that this new year is going to be all about me, probably for the first time in my life."

"That sounds like a good plan."

"I don't know. I feel like we have both grown as humans the past week, you know? I know you left a long-term relationship, and so did I, both of them riddled with cheating. And maybe my sister was right, fate did lead us here to be together and to heal each other."

"You think that's what's happening?" His voice seems a little skeptical.

"Yeah, I do. I feel like you have made me stronger, and more confident in myself. Rob took that away from me, and I didn't realize how much until being here with you." A small tear falls down my cheek which Luke rubs away with his thumb.

"Lilly ..." My name is a whisper on his lips.

"I'm being silly, I know."

He shakes his head. "Crazily enough, I understand."

"You do?"

"Yeah. For the first time in who knows how long, I'm able to breathe, relax, and put myself first without worrying about repercussions."

"Not to sound too corny, but it's like we're both on a journey."

Luke's hand wraps around my neck and pulls me closer to him, his lips feather-soft against my own. "I'm so glad to have met you."

"Me, too."

He kisses me ever so softly. "I'd like us to be friends." His agreement stings a little, even though that's what I asked for. *What did you think he was going to profess his undying love for you after one week?*

"I don't think I want you out of my life." His kisses turn heated.

Before things can turn any hotter with his hand under my sleep shirt and his fingers plucking at my nipples, my phone rings. Groaning, I run into the bedroom to grab it. My stomach sinks when I see who's calling. Mom and Dad.

Shit. I suck in a deep breath and try to calm myself, try to channel some of that newfound confidence I had only a few moments earlier.

"Merry Christmas, guys," I answer the phone happily.

They sent me a text wishing me, 'Happy greetings,' and that was it.

"Christmas was days ago, Lilly," Dad chastises me.

"We just got off from a distressing phone call from Rob's parents, Lilly. Care to explain?" Mom questions me. I'm on speakerphone, so this isn't good.

"Did you hear the news that Laura and Andy got engaged?" I attempt to change the subject to something a little lighter.

"Yes. It's nice to see one of our girls is doing something right," Mom adds.

Wow. That barb stings. I screw up my nose as tears begin to well in my eyes.

Keep it together, Lilly.

"I can't believe you left your fiancé in Africa ... without telling him," Dad adds incredulously, the disappointment dripping through his comment.

"So, what version of events did Rob's family give you?" Fuck Rob and his pompous family, this is *not* my fault. "I mean, someone just doesn't pack up and move halfway across the world if they are in a happy relationship, do they?"

Silence falls between us all.

"Rob indicated he is very much in the dark," my father adds.

"Well, let me enlighten you both."

"You don't have to take that tone with us, Lilly. We're the ones upset here," Mom adds.

Oh, for fuck's sake, my blood begins to boil.

"Let me tell you about Vivian, the French nurse who I caught him screwing behind my tent." Mom gasps down the line. "Or what about Francesca, the Italian nurse, or Lala, the Spanish nurse ... oh, and then there was Darla, the American soldier. Who else was there?" I tap my finger against my chin. "Oh, that's right, Jana, the Australian refugee worker. I know there were more, but honestly, I think that's enough, don't you?"

"Don't be so crude, Lilly," my father yells at me. "Robert comes from a good home. He'd never do something like that."

"Why the hell would I make it up?" I raise my voice at his disbelieving tone.

"If it were true, surely you would've said something earlier, sweetheart," Mom tries to placate me.

My raised voice must have alerted Luke to my argument because he's standing looking utterly concerned for me. Just seeing him there gives me the strength I need to continue, "You made sure you raised a woman who wouldn't say anything. You raised a woman that even though her entire world was crumbling around her, that her heart had been ripped out of her chest, that she was utterly humiliated on a daily basis knowing the entire camp knew her fiancé was fucking every woman with a pulse, that she'd take it with a fucking smile on her face. Either of you know the reason why?" Before they get a chance to answer, I state, "Because she was so damn scared to disappoint you both."

"Do not use that foul language," Dad adds.

"That's what you're concerned about?" I say. Tears are falling fast now, and as soon as the first teardrop falls down my cheek and drips off, Luke is beside me, linking his hand with mine. "You're worried about the use of the word *fuck,* not that your daughter's fiancé has been cheating on her from the moment we touched down in Africa."

"Robert has a very stressful job, sweetheart," Mom adds.

Is this woman fucking serious?

"We do the same fucking job. Actually, I'm the one who graduated from university with honors, not him."

"It's not a competition, Lilly," Dad adds.

I've never wanted to punch anything more than I do right now.

"And yet, you want me to marry a cheating asshole so *you* will look better to all your friends."

"I can't deal with her," Dad yells down the phone. I hear his footsteps fading into the distance.

"Rob made a mistake, sweetheart. He's young and handsome. He probably got caught up in the adventure of it and took it too far."

Is my mom delusional?

"And that makes it okay?" Maybe now we are woman to woman, she'll get me.

"No, it doesn't, sweetie." *Ah, finally.* "But, in all honesty, you're not going to do any better than him." Her words are like a dagger to the heart—my own mother has just split my heart in two. "Maybe some time apart will do you both good. Once Rob's finished sowing his wild oats, you can be together."

"No."

"Excuse me?"

I don't think I have ever said no to my parents before.

"I said … no. Rob and I are done. I'll courier the engagement ring back to them."

"Lilly, think about what you're saying." She sounds panicked, and I can imagine she's twisting her hair around her finger and pulling. "You're going to ruin our reputation."

"I don't care." She gasps down the line. "What about me? What about what I deserve? You're more worried about your society friends than your own daughter. You would rather I live a horrible life with a man I don't love, who'll never stay faithful to me, just because it makes *you* look good. I've only now realized just how selfish the two of you are."

"How dare you speak to us like that. We're your parents," Mom seethes down the phone line.

"No, you're not because a real parent would not sell their child off because it benefits them."

"You'll be disinherited if you continue down this path, Lilly," my mother threatens me.

"I don't care." She gasps, obviously surprised at my answer.

"And guess what? I'm disinheriting you. Never call me again." And with those words spoken, I hang up the phone and stare at it for the longest time, just blinking.

"Are you okay, Lilly?" Luke gently asks.

That's when I lose it completely.

15

LUCA

"**H**ey," Lilly answers the phone in her bedroom on speaker. She hasn't been her bubbly self since her phone call with her parents. As soon as she hung up, she crumbled as if everything had finally caught up with her. I held her as she cried herself to sleep while feeling utterly helpless. But I was going to be there for her no matter what. That's what friends do, and I was determined to be the best. While Lilly slept, I sent Laura an email telling her what happened and that she should call her because I doubt her parents were calling Laura to tell her what happened.

"God, I hate our parents," Laura grumbles.

"It's not their fault, they suck." Lilly still tries to find the good in her parents after what they just did to her.

"To say the things they said to you … it's unforgivable."

"It is what it is."

She sounds defeated.

"Maybe we should come home?" Laura asks.

"What? No. You're not packing up and coming home to look after my pathetic ass."

There is nothing pathetic about Lilly.

"You just don't want us to cramp your style with your Italian Stallion."

Say what now? Italian Stallion?

"Shhh, Laura. You're on speaker, he might hear you."

Laura laughs. "I'm still waiting for a photo of him."

Why does she want a photo of me?

"No way. I've told you that." Lilly laughs.

"You haven't been chopped up into little bits yet, but as I said, it's security just in case something happens to you."

That's morbid as fuck.

Mental note—send a photograph to Laura to ease her mind.

"Well, it would be your fault for not doing the proper checks before hightailing it to Africa."

It's nice hearing her laugh again.

"Well, I didn't think my sister would be sharing a cottage with the stranger I rented it to, now did I?" Laura comments through her laughter.

"What are your plans for the new year?" Lilly asks.

"We're off on a safari to Botswana. Like camping in the wild with lions and stuff," Laura says excitedly.

"That sounds amazing. You're going to have the best time."

"What about you? Does the Italian Stallion have plans?" Laura asks.

No, I do not. I just thought we'd stay here and ring in the new year naked.

"We'll probably just stay in."

"Booo," Laura yells. "You should be ringing in the new year in style. Go to Edinburgh, do Hogmanay there."

"Edinburgh is sold out a year in advance for New Year's Eve. Plus, I can't just drag Luke to Edinburgh when he has booked the cottage for his holiday."

Why can't she? I'd go.

That gives me an idea. I should be using my connections.

What's the point of being me if it doesn't come with its advantages?

"Go by yourself then. It's not like you're dating him. You are single ... ready to mingle."

I do not like the sound of Laura's suggestion.

"I'm not ready."

"I understand. But, babe, please have fun. Forget about Mom and Dad. This is your fresh start."

"Thanks. I can't wait to hug you when you get home."

"Me, too. Happy New Year, Lilly."

"Happy New Year, Lolly."

16

LUCA

Lilly has no idea about the surprise I have planned. After eavesdropping in on her conversation with her sister, Laura gave me the perfect idea to cheer Lilly up and say thank you for everything. She doesn't know how much she's made me think about things. I mean, let's be honest, outside of fucking her, eating, and playing Monopoly, there isn't anything else to do but be with your thoughts. I spent the day googling everything about New Year's Eve in Edinburgh. There's a castle where they have a huge fireworks display. It looks cool and something totally out of my comfort zone. I made a couple of calls, and voilà, we're all booked in.

"Why do you have a creepy smile on your face?" Lilly asks as she looks up at me from her place by the fire where she likes to read her book.

"I have a surprise for you."

She raises her eyebrows. "Really?" Her eyes drift to my dick, he twitches under her gaze.

"Eyes up here," I tease. "You can thank him later, but right now, I'm taking you away."

"Away!" She raises her voice.

"Yes. You and I are going away somewhere special for tonight." I can see she wants to argue, but she's genuinely shocked. "Go … get changed. I have packed a bag for you."

"You did what?"

Did I overstep the mark with my surprise?

"I wanted to surprise you."

"I am," she says and the next thing I know, she rushes over to me and plants a kiss on my cheek. "Oh my god, I'm so excited." With that, she rushes out of the room to get changed, and I laugh.

"Are you ready?" I ask a short time later as we jump into the 4WD.

"Yes." She nervously bounces one of her legs up and down repeatedly. "No one has spontaneously booked a holiday for me before. Even if it's for one night."

"We're going to have one crazy New Year's Eve, Lilly. We are going to bring in the year of being selfish."

"Hell, yes," she replies, then claps her hands excitedly.

According to the map, Edinburgh is about three hours away, but the drive is through a heap of mountains, so it will probably take us a while to get there. Ever the guide, Lilly gives me a history lesson as we go. We stop at some quaint little villages on the way to look around. As much as I tell her we're in a hurry, she is having way too much fun, and as long as we make it there before midnight, I'm fine with however long it takes.

The level of comfort I feel around her, I have never felt with another woman. Maybe, I've always let whatever I have with a woman be very superficial, but our situation has made it deeper and more meaningful. I mean, we have literally been stuck in the tiniest of cottages for the holidays—how could we not get to know each other on a basic level.

There's only so much fucking you can do.

There I've said it—take my man card.

I have been thinking more and more about Lilly's question regarding being friends after this is all over. Can we just be friends? I mean, it's going to be hard not imagining her naked every time I'm around her, but it's better than not having her in my life at all.

That could still happen, though, when she finds out who you are. She'll understand, won't she?

I mean, it doesn't define me. I'm still the same man, it's just my job isn't exactly what I told her it was. Technically, I haven't lied. *Yes, you have.*

Pushing those thoughts away, I concentrate on the here and now because, in this moment, I know Lilly likes me for me.

"What's going on in that big old head of yours? You seem incredibly quiet all of a sudden?" Lilly asks as she reaches out and links her hand with mine.

Looking over at her, I see her light brown hair is pulled up into a high ponytail. She's wearing no makeup, and her cheeks are pink from the winter wind at our last stop.

"Isn't that my question to you?"

"Seems like I've been rubbing off on you." She smiles brightly at me, her blue eyes shimmering with happiness.

"I like it when you rub off on me." My innuendo makes her blush. "I like you."

"I like you, too."

"Good."

She frowns. "That's all?" She pushes me for more.

"I've been thinking about what you said the other day about being friends." She stiffens slightly. "I want that ... you and me to be friends." Her face lights up, and it's fantastic to watch. "I can't guarantee I won't stop flirting with you, though," I warn her.

"You're Italian, it's in your blood to flirt." She smirks.

"True. Beautiful women are our weakness." This makes her chuckle. "I'm glad you stumbled in on me naked."

"Me, too," she agrees, squeezing my hand. "Let's make this the best New Year's Eve, friend."

I know what she meant when she used the word 'friend' but not going to lie, it stung. *Have I ever been friend-zoned?* I mean, we'll still be sleeping with each other for a couple more weeks, but after that, there will be nothing.

It's not even like I could want more. No matter how much I may want it, my family would never accept Lilly. For one, she isn't Italian. *She is fluent in Italian, though.* Two, she isn't from the right breeding. *Right, because the right breeding didn't just humiliate me in public.*

Stop thinking about them. Just enjoy this for what it is, Luca, a holiday romance.

I booked us a luxury penthouse with views over Edinburgh Castle and the city. I asked for discretion when I arrived because of who I am. I know if I hadn't, they would've made a huge fuss, and as far as Lilly is concerned, I'm just a businessman.

We pull up at the back entrance where a valet is waiting for us. I tell him we'll take our own bags. He hands me the key to the penthouse and quietly drives off to park my car.

"Wow, this place is amazing."

Seeing the awe on Lilly's face is amazing. She has no idea I can show her so much. I could whisk her away to some of my favorite places—Monaco, New York, and the Greek Islands. We could explore the world—I want to see it all again through her eyes. I'd love to see how she'd fit into my world. Would she think it's over the top, or would she appreciate it?

It's never going to happen. I know, but I man can hope.

"Oh my god, this view," she say as she presses her face against the glass. We have almost a three-sixty-degree view over the entire city. "We're going to be able to see all the fireworks from here. This is going to be spectacular." The excitement she's exuding vibrates through her body.

"What I see is a beautiful woman standing against a window. One I want to press her naked body against."

She turns around slowly, the blush is back across those cheeks. "I don't think anyone needs to see that," she whispers.

"You're right. I'd never share you with the world," I tell her, pulling her face to mine and kissing her hard.

Lilly's fingers are in my hair in an instant, tugging at the ends, and our kiss grows frantic as we strip off the winter layers—scarves, jumpers, T-shirts, jeans, socks—all discarded onto the floor. Thankfully, the fire is on in the living room, and there's a large fur rug on the floor where I place her gently as I shimmy off her underwear. Lightly, I push open her legs for me. I have done this so many times that Lilly instinctively opens for me now, and I reward her for her eagerness with my tongue across her silky slit.

"Hmmm," Lilly moans as her fingers find my hair again, tugging the dark strands and pulling me closer to her. I follow her instructions, feasting on her as if I'm a starving man. Showing her what life could be like with me. How I'd love her every single day.

"Yes, yes ... oh God, yes." She arches her back as the orgasm takes her over.

My hand is pulling out a condom from discarded jeans pocket. I know I should love her more, but I need to be inside her and connected with her. Once I'm sheathed, I enter her slowly, and she rewards me by wrapping her legs around me. I hiss as I feel her wetness surround me.

"You and me," I whisper, pressing our foreheads together.

"You and me." She smiles, then kisses me.

17

LUCA

L illy is beyond excited, especially because she can stay in her pajamas and not have to dodge the crowds. It's beginning to sleet as well. They must be freezing down on the streets, and here we are drinking wine and eating delicious food which has been laid out thanks to the in-house chef. This is the perfect New Year's Eve—no responsibilities, no pomp, no paparazzi, just me and a crazy English girl who's squealing at everything she sees out the window. How can you not get caught up in the excitement of this night?

"Everything is so awesome," Lilly says as she comes away from the window long enough to grab a few pieces of cheese and a cracker.

"It certainly is. I had no idea there'd be so many people," I comment. There has to be hundreds of thousands of people on the street in the freezing weather.

"I've always wanted to do this, but it's always seemed way too expensive. This must have cost you a small fortune. I mean … this view is unbelievable."

"I do okay," is all I tell her as she sits on my lap.

"Well, thank you. I appreciate it." She kisses my cheek.

Has a woman ever thanked me for a gift before? The genuine thanks that's written all over Lilly's face, have I ever seen that before? It's always expected that I'll shower the women I'm with in expensive things. I've never noticed until now.

A phone rings, and Lilly rushes over to it. "Lolly," she squeals. "You're never going to guess where I am?" I can hear it in her tone, just how happy she is to hear from her sister. "Luke whisked me away to Edinburgh for New Year's Eve."

I wonder if Laura's okay that I have done this.

"I know. It's so awesome. Our apartment looks over the castle, and I can see everyone in the streets. It's freezing, and I'm wearing my PJs. Best New Year's Eve ever."

"Okay, Lolly. Love you, bye."

"She's having fun?" I ask her.

"The very best. They are about to go out on safari," she tells me.

"You miss it?" I ask about Africa.

"A little. The break has been good, helped sort through things. I know I'm not going to give up being a doctor. Just not sure where to start my new life."

"I know some people in the charity world ..." silence falls between us, "... I could put in some calls to some people I know in Italy."

"Italy?"

"Yes, but I'm sure they have charities in other places around the world. It doesn't have to be Italy."

"You would do that for me?"

"We're friends, of course," I answer with a shrug. I mean, in my world it's all about who you know. Plus, I'm owed many favors. "You don't have to decide now. I can find out where they need help and let you know."

"Thank you. Thank you so much, Luke," she says, genuinely touched by my offer. Tears begin to well in her eyes, and I wipe them away. I don't know many women who would be moved to tears by my offering to help them find a job.

"Hey, no tears. Not on New Year's Eve," I tell her.

"I feel like meeting you was the best thing that could've ever happened to me," she says as she pulls me into a hug, a very non-sexual hug, more a hug of gratitude.

"I'd do anything for you, Lilly. You're a good person."

"You're not so bad yourself," she says as we clink our glasses of champagne together.

＊＊＊＊

Three …

Two …

One …

We're cuddled together after popping a bottle of champagne and waiting for the fireworks to commence. A kaleidoscope of color and smoke fills the night sky around the castle.

"Happy New Year, Lilly."

"Happy New Year, Luke."

We celebrate midnight with a passionate kiss, then our attention is pulled back to the fireworks display in front of us. Lilly oohs and aahs as each rocket fills the black sky with reds, greens, gold, and so many colors it's spectacular.

I am so happy I'm sharing this night with her and starting a new year with her.

All I know is, I might not be able to walk away from her when my time is up at the cottage.

＊＊＊＊

There's banging on the door. Who the hell is banging on our door at this time of the morning? I look over at the bedside table

—it's 10:37 a.m. on New Year's Day. The apartment better be on fire, otherwise, heads will roll.

"Who is it?" Lilly asks croakily from beside me.

"I have no idea." I rub my eyes.

"They seem very insistent," she says.

I pull on my sweatpants, and Lilly does the same. I stride through the apartment, annoyed that some inconsiderate person is waking us up so early. I pull open the door in my irritated state.

"What!" I shout.

My eyes focus on the people standing in front of me—my sister and my ex plus a legion of bodyguards.

"What the hell are you doing here?" I scream at them in Italian.

"Happy New Year to you, too, brother," Allegra says stiffly. Her eyes glance over my shoulder at the movement behind me. "Didn't take you long to find some whore to keep you entertained."

I take a step toward her. Never in my life have I ever wanted to hurt my sister like I do right now. How dare she call Lilly a whore.

Allegra pushes her way into the apartment with her entourage in tow. "I see your standards have dropped."

"I see your manners have disappeared also," Lilly replies back in perfect Italian.

Which gives them all pause.

Allegra looks over at Lilly, and I can see the sneer that's curling on her lip. "Who are you?" she demands, folding her arms across her chest.

Lilly looks behind her and sees Rachele, my ex, and their bodyguards.

"Does it really matter who I am?" Lilly replies. She looks like she's about to blow a fuse.

Walking over to where Lilly is currently standing, I place my hand in hers.

Lilly's shaking, but she's holding it together well.

"No, it doesn't. You're just one of many of Luca's conquests. Don't get too comfortable," Allegra snips at her again.

"Luca?" Lilly whispers.

I squeeze her hand, and her attention is drawn back to the two women in front of her.

"I think you've proved your point, Luca. Now come home, so we can get married," Rachele adds, her eyes glaring furiously at Lilly.

"Married?" Lilly gasps as she drops my hand like it's on fire.

"Oh, did my brother forget to tell you that? He was supposed to get married just before Christmas. He left my poor friend here at the altar." The smile on Allegra's face says she knows she's found Lilly's weakness.

"He's my fiancé, whore," Rachele adds.

The harsh words hit Lilly, and she takes a step back, blinking fast trying to keep tears at bay. Does she not remember me telling her I was cheated on?

I knew my family would eventually come and mess everything up.

"The only whore I see is standing in front of me. You fucked my best man at our rehearsal dinner," I yell at Rachele who has the sense to flinch at my words.

"Please, as if you weren't sleeping with other women." Allegra rolls her eyes.

"I wasn't," I shout, thumping my chest. "I thought …" I let the words trail off until Allegra and Rachele burst out laughing.

"Oh, dear brother, you seriously thought you would be getting married for love." *How hard is that to believe in?* "You know who we are. We must marry for connections, not love." My sister chuckles as if it is idiotic for me to think I deserve love.

"I thought we had an understanding," Rachele adds. "I had no idea …" She tries to contain her laughter.

"Who are you?" Lilly asks as she turns to me, a frown marring her beautiful face.

"You haven't told her?" Allegra jabs. "Oh, that's cute. You wanted to slum it and be a commoner?"

I can see the distress written on her face, and I don't like it one little bit. "What's she saying, Luke?"

"You're even using a commoner's name. Luke … how bouji." My sister's cackles fill the apartment.

"Luke, Luca, whoever you are," Lilly says.

"I'm still me, Lilly," I say, reaching out to her trying to keep the connection we had earlier.

"He is Principe Luca Fiorenzo," my sister explains.

"You're a prince?" Lilly says as she looks at me in shock.

"Yes, but …" I start to explain.

Lilly pulls her arm away from my reach. "Why didn't you tell me? Why did you lie? You told me you were a businessman." The hurt on Lilly's face is palpable.

"That's all true. I'm a businessman, but I am also a prince."

"A prince who needs a princess. One that he has been betrothed to since birth," Allegra adds.

Fuck her. "I don't want Rachele," I spit.

"You would rather that?" Rachele asks as she gives a dissatisfied glance at Lilly.

"You know nothing about me. I'm a doctor and certainly not a damn whore. I've just arrived back from saving lives in Africa. I grew up surrounded by royals and London's elite. My parents are doctors to most of them," Lilly points out. "What do you do with your time? Spend it shopping? Going to parties? Cheating on your fiancé? Now, look in the mirror and see who's lacking."

"You bitch," Rachele spits as she launches herself at Lilly.

I quickly push her behind me and stop my raging ex before

she touches her. The bodyguards pull Rachele off me, but not without her scratching my face first.

"How dare you," she screams like a wild cat.

Lilly smiles at them both, knowing she has secretly won because that's exactly what they do all day, shop and attend parties.

Allegra turns and glares at me. "If you won't come back for her, then come back for Papà."

"What?"

"Papà had a heart attack while you were away. I guess it was the public disgrace of his son not arriving on his wedding day that did him in. It's all your fault," Allegra shouts at me.

My entire world stops. "What? No. I don't believe you. Giorgio would've told me. I only spoke to him the other day."

"He didn't have it on your wedding day, but he had it a couple of days ago. Knowing you missed Christmas and now New Year's. Those are holidays we never miss together, no matter what," Allegra explains to me.

Is that sincerity in my sister's voice? "Is he okay?" I ask as my hands shake because as much as I hate the control my family exercises over me, they are still my family.

"He's in the hospital," she informs me.

The world falls out beneath me. This is serious. What have I done? My leaving has put my father in the hospital.

Lilly places a hand on me. "You should go … be with your family, Luca," she says, using my real name.

We still have a couple of weeks together. What we have can't be ending now. I've only just found her. But I must go and see my father, tell him I'm sorry for causing him stress. I didn't mean to. I needed to think. I needed time to wrap my head around my fiancée's betrayal. After this little stunt she's pulled, we are done. I'm disgusted by her and Allegra too. Will Lilly come back home with me? I'm not ready to say goodbye. *Do you think she wants to be involved in the shitstorm that is brewing back there?* The media will paint her out to be the woman who broke Rachele and me up, and I know her camp will spin it like that. Rachele will stand there with fake tears in her eyes telling the world I broke her heart and ran away with Lilly. I can't do that to her.

I turn and look at my sister. "Give us a moment."

She glares at me but takes her entourage with her out of the apartment.

"You need to go be with your family, Luca. Don't worry about me, I'll be fine," she says, trying to reassure me, but the way her arms are wrapped around her as if she is hugging herself tells me otherwise.

"Come ... come with me?" I ask. Hope. Beg. Plead.

She shakes her head. "Now isn't the time to worry them with anything or anyone else," she says unable to look at me.

"What about us?" I ask as I grab her face, making her look at me.

"Everything's changed, Luca," she says as tears stream down her cheeks.

"No. No, it hasn't."

"We were only meant to be a holiday romance, nothing more," she says quietly.

My heart begins to break as a sick feeling develops deep in my stomach. "No. Fate had other plans for us. I've fallen for you, Lilly."

She pushes herself out of my arms and paces the room. "You may think you have, but we come from two vastly different worlds. I'm just someone you thought you wanted, but in the end, I'll be a nice story to remember when you're old," she tells me angrily.

"Never. You mean so much more to me than a fucking story, Lilly. You can't stand there and tell me you have no feelings for me whatsoever."

Lilly stills and I can see the moment she decides to break my heart. "How can I? I don't know who you are." Her words cut like a knife to my chest.

Me being who I am shouldn't change things that much. "I'm still me, Lilly. The same guy who stood naked in your cottage living room. The same guy who thinks you're the most beautiful woman in the world. The same guy who wants so desperately for the woman he realizes he loves to love him back."

Yes, love. There, I said it because I know what I feel for her is real and true. It's nothing I've ever experienced with anyone else and as bad as it sounds, I've experienced a lot of women. She is the first woman that made me feel like I was home.

Lilly looks up at me through red-rimmed eyes. "I think you have me confused with someone else."

She doesn't love me. My heart breaks at that realization. I thought there might be a chance, even if it's been quick that she felt that connection between us. That she could see herself falling for me too.

I stare at her, really stare at her, and she does the same back at me. "Tell me you don't love me, and I'll go."

"Luca," Lilly says, hiccupping through her tears.

No, I won't listen to whatever bullshit she is about to sprout to me. "You feel it too, I know you do." I plead with her to give me a sign that I'm not alone in this.

She shakes her head. "It was just fun."

Liar. She's lying. Why is she being so fucking stubborn? "I don't believe you."

Lilly looks up at me and anger falls across her face. "I don't care if you believe me or not. I know what I feel, and I feel nothing for you."

My heart aches as her words hit their target. She's serious. I can see it written all over her face. She doesn't love me. I truly was a rebound, a good time for her while she got over her own heartbreak. I thought, no I hoped things were different. I was wrong.

Straightening my back, I look up at her. "The job offer still stands. I've already contacted my friend. So, you will be hearing from him about working for his charity. You can do good in his world, don't say no to his offer because of me," I tell her.

She gives me a small nod in understanding.

That's it then. This is it. The end. I turn on my heel, head to the bedroom, and shove my stuff into my overnight bag, which doesn't take me too long to do. When I emerge from the bedroom Lilly is staring out the big picture window overlooking the city. Her shoulders shake as she tries to hide the fact that she's crying. I can't leave her like this.

Dropping my bag to the floor, I rush toward her. "Lilly," I call her name, and she turns just as I reach her. Next thing I know, I am pulling her into my arms and kissing her. I put everything I feel for her into that kiss. One last attempt to see if she might love me back even the tiniest bit. She kisses me back urgently, but her kisses feel like she is saying goodbye, I can taste her salty tears.

I tear myself away from her, and as soon as there is distance between us, she turns and stares out the window again. It feels like walking through wet cement every step away from her.

It doesn't feel right. It feels like I'm making the biggest mistake of my life, but I can't force someone to love me back.

"The keys for the car are on the table. Someone will come and collect the car after you get home," I say as I sadly walk out of the apartment not knowing when or if I'll ever see Lilly again.

18

LILLY

I t's a long journey home by myself. Thankfully, he left me his 4WD after he'd gone. Otherwise, I would have no idea how I'd be getting home. I pick up my phone and call the only person I know who will understand. It rings and rings and rings until it drops out, so I try again.

"Lilly." Laura's voice echoes through the car's speakers, and I burst into tears. "Lil, what's the matter? Has something happened?"

"Luke. Lied to me."

"He did what?" Laura asks.

"He lied. His name isn't Luke. His real name is Prince Luca Fiorenzo," I tell her.

Laura giggles. "Did you say prince?"

"Yes," I say through my sniffles.

The phone falls silent.

"You're being serious?" she asks.

"Yes, and his evil sister and fiancée have just dragged him home to Italy," I say, hiccupping through my tears.

"He has a fiancée?" Laura's voice raises.

"He left her at the altar because she slept with his best man at his rehearsal dinner," I explain.

"She did what?!"

"They called me a whore." I understand I'm giving my sister the cliffs notes version of what's just happened. I'm slightly traumatized by everything, and I think in shock too. This was not at all how I saw the start of my new year going.

"Oh, hell, no. She doesn't get to call my sister a whore and walk away scot-free. The audacity to call you that when she's the one screwing her fiancé's friend," Laura yells down the phone. "They are so lucky that I wasn't there. Royalty or not, I'd have kicked their regal asses."

This makes me chuckle as I would have liked to see that. "I would've paid money to see you try. Don't worry, I stuck up for myself."

"Good for you. So, where's Luke now?"

"Luca ... he went back to Italy," I explain to her.

"He left you? Oh, hell, no ... damn! I need to kick his ass as well," she yells.

"His father had a heart attack and is in the hospital. That's why they were trying to find him," I add.

"Oh. Doesn't that seem a little too convenient?" Laura seers.

"Laura! Don't say that," I tell her while shaking my head.

"Well, they sound like bitches. I wouldn't put it past women like that. I've watched *The Tudors* ... royalty does that sort of shit."

"This isn't medieval times, Laura," I say, shaking my head.

"So, what are you going to do?"

"Nothing," I tell her. There isn't anything I can do. It was fun while it lasted, but we are over.

"Nothing? You're just going to let a prince go?" my sister questions me.

"I don't care that he's a prince."

"I know, but still, a prince," she says.

I look out over the white rolling hills of the Scottish country-side and try to picture myself living in a gilded castle. *No. I don't think that's for me.*

"He told me he loves me," I tell her.

A squeal echoes through the car. "He what? Why would you leave the most important thing out of the story? He loves you …." She squeals.

My tears flow thinking about the way he kissed me as he said goodbye. The way he tried to convince me that what he was feeling was real.

And I pushed him away. There was no point, there's no future between us. We come from two entirely different worlds. "I told him to leave."

"Oh, Lilly-poo. Why would you do that?" My sister's voice softens.

"Because it was the right thing to do. We can never work. His sister made it abundantly clear I was beneath her, and by the sounds of it, his whole family would feel the same way. I get enough of that from our parents," I tell her, letting out a long sigh.

"Once they get to know you, they'll love you. How can they not? You're frickin' awesome," Laura states.

"I think it's for the best."

There's a long pause before Laura speaks again. "Do you love him?" she asks.

"We've only known each other for a couple of weeks, the world doesn't work like that," I tell her.

"Bullshit, and you still didn't answer the question. Do you love him?" she pushes.

Do I love him? I don't know. No. Liar. *You have fallen head over heels for that man.* Doesn't matter. I live in the real world not a fairytale. Love doesn't conquer all in the real world, and the handsome prince doesn't fall for the commoner doctor.

"It doesn't matter. His life is there, and mine is ... somewhere but not there," I tell her.

"Lilly, you deserve to be loved," Laura tells me.

"And I am, by you."

"That's sisterly love which is different to soulmate love."

Not this again. I love my sister, but sometimes she is too hippy for my conservative brain.

"Fate works in mysterious ways. She brought you the perfect man, but it wasn't the right time. But she wanted to show you that you had been settling with Rob and that you were worthy of so much more. So, she gave you Luke."

If fate works like that, then she's a bitch because that was a low thing to do to me. Dangle that delicious Italian carrot in my face then cruelly snatch it away.

"Forget about the disaster that is my life and go enjoy yours. I love you. And I can't wait to see you again," I tell my sister. I don't want to ruin her wonderful holiday with my drama.

"Love you, Lilly. Just remember ... you *are* worth it."

And with that bit of wisdom, she hangs up.

19

LUCA

The flight back to Italy was a tense one. I didn't care about anything Rachele and Allegra had to say. I simply needed to see Papà and make sure he was okay. When we finally made it to the hospital, I spent the entire day by my father's bedside with my family. It was horrible seeing him lying in bed not moving. He's usually so full of energy and joy, that to see him like this is worrying. The doctors have reassured us that he is going to make a full recovery, but he does have to change some things in his diet which my father isn't so keen on.

"Need some company?" Natalia, my youngest sister, links her arm with mine as we arrive back home.

"Not really," I tell her not wanting to be rude, but it's been a day from hell.

"I know, but you're still going to get it," she says, giving me a blinding smile.

I'm too exhausted to fight her. We continue through my family's home in silence. I keep an apartment there, it's my old childhood bedroom, but it's easier sometimes to stay here than travel back across the city to my apartment sometimes.

Natalia walks me back to my room and stops at the door. "Go have a shower and freshen up and then meet me downstairs."

"I'm not in the mood, Natalia."

"I know, but you have no choice," she says, being annoying as she gives me those puppy dog eyes, and I can't say no to her.

"Fine," I grumble.

"Thought so," she says as she turns on her heels and skips back down the corridor.

Shaking my head, I step back into my room and slowly undress, leaving a pile of clothes in my wake.

As I step into the shower and the water hits me, I realize I am washing Lilly off me. With each stroke across my skin, she gets further and further away. *It's for the best.* Maybe it is, she's just moved halfway across the world because of her cheating fiancé, and I did the same. There might be some truth in what Lilly said about fate, that maybe we were both destined to meet each other in that cottage and heal each other in that moment and nothing more. No. What I feel for Lilly seems so much stronger than a rebound fling. My feelings for her are real, and I won't have anyone tell me otherwise. Just wished she felt the same.

"You look better after that shower," Natalia tells me while handing me a coffee.

I take a sip of the dark liquid and groan. *Oh, how I've missed thee.*

"Guessing they didn't have good coffee where you were?" She chuckles.

"Only instant," I tell her.

She screws up her face at the thought. "So, where were you? Giorgio and I couldn't find you at all, but somehow, Allegra was able to."

That's what I haven't been able to work out, how the hell Allegra found me so easily. I guess knowing my sister, she probably paid off the right people.

"Are you really surprised by anything she does?" I say as I take another sip of coffee and savor it.

"No, not really. It was weird she took Rachele with her, though?" Natalia suggests.

"That's because they knew I was with someone," I confess to her.

Natalia's eyes widen. "You work fast, brother."

I can hear the tone in her voice rise—it's in a non-approval pitch.

Pulling out my phone, I hand it to her, showing her the only picture of Lilly and me that we took. We're dressed in our pajamas, sipping champagne, enjoying the night blissfully unaware that it was about to go up in flames the next morning.

Natalia stares at the photograph for a long moment. "You look really happy," she says as she hands me back my phone.

"I was. For the first time … someone liked me … for me," I tell her.

"She didn't know who you were?"

"Not until Allegra and Rachele arrived," I explain.

"And?" she questions.

"She didn't want me." Remembering the hurt on Lilly's face when she learned the truth about who I was, it's seared into my memory.

"Wait! What? She turned you down?" Natalia can't believe it.

"Yes."

"Okay, you're going to have to start from the beginning," she says, leaning in closer waiting for me to spill what happened.

So, I do.

I tell her about how we met, which she thought was hilarious. I told her about how she was a doctor in Africa and about her ex. How she took me to the pub for Christmas Eve, then made me an Italian Christmas dinner. I told her about our epic Monopoly sessions and our hike in the snow. About the times we sat beside the fire, not having to fill the silence because it was comfortable.

"Sounds like you have feelings for this girl?" Natalia questions.

"I do. I …" Scrubbing my hands across my face, I continue, "… I told her I loved her as I left, and she told me she didn't feel the same." I hang my head between my hands. "She hasn't answered any of my texts or calls since I left."

"It sounds like a lot was sprung on her all at once. Plus, she had the demon twins attacking her on all fronts at the same time." *They were horrible to Lilly, that's for sure.* "She might have said she didn't feel anything for you to save face, especially with Allegra and Rachele around."

Hope begins to blossom in my chest. "You think?"

"I think all you can do is give her time." Natalia reaches out and laces her hand with mine. "Your face lights up when you talk about her. I have never seen that reaction from you before."

"She's different," I confess to my sister.

"But is she worth it, Luca? You know our parents want you to marry Rachele. They have it all planned."

"Do they know about what she did?" I ask.

Natalia shakes her head. "No. Allegra and Rachele spun some story to them, and then Papà started to feel ill. So Giorgio and I didn't want to push it. We thought you would be back at Christmas, but when that came and went, Papà kept getting worst."

"Fuck! It's all my fault."

Natalia shakes her head. "No, don't say that. Papà likes to drink too much red wine and eat too much cheese. You know Mama has wanted him to cut down on his vices, but he hasn't listened," she reassures me.

"I've added to his stress, though."

"I blame Allegra and Rachele, not you. Rachele needs to

remember to keep her legs together instead of fucking Marcus behind your back," she says angrily.

"Where's Marcus?" I ask. Some friend he was fucking my fiancée behind my back. I wonder what happened to my best friend of twenty-seven years, he's suspiciously quiet. I thought he would be calling and groveling.

"South of France somewhere. I will say, he did apologize to Giorgio and me about everything. He told us that he and Rachele had been fooling around for years on and off. He said he'd broken things off with her, and she told him she wanted to end their relationship with one last fuck before getting married." Natalia gives me an apologetic look.

"I hated him when it first happened. I didn't understand how he could do this to me. That he would blow up our lifelong friendship like he did," I say on a sigh. Then I look down at my phone at the picture of Lilly and me and smile. "I think I should be thanking him. If he hadn't done what he did, I'd have married Rachele and been none the wiser."

"I would've tried to help you annul it," my sister tells me.

Of course, she would have.

"Am I crazy for falling for a woman after such a short time?" I ask her.

"No way in the world. It's romantic. Such a meet cute," she says with a wide smile.

Meet cute? What the hell is that?

"Sounds like the two of you were the right people at the right time for each other. I thought when you got back from wherever you were, you would be an unbearable grump. But I'm happy that you're not," she says.

"Feels like my heart's been ripped out of my chest though," I tell her.

"Aw. You're such a romantic. That's weird because you never spoke like that with Rachele."

"Didn't feel for Rachele what I do for Lilly," I confess.

"The heart wants what the heart wants, brother. It's all going to work out in the end. Lilly will come back to you when it's time."

"You think?" I ask, feeling slightly optimistic.

"Give Lilly some space. She has her own baggage, and you've dumped some more on her. She's probably shell-shocked over it all especially when she thought you were one person, but in reality, you are another."

"I was still me, just my name changed," I argue.

"A lie is a lie, brother. She is going to be upset for a while so be patient with her. If you feel this strongly about her then you're going to have to have patience," she explains.

When did my little sister become so wise?

"What do I do then?"

"Wait. But don't ghost her. She may not want to talk to you, but she'll still like hearing from you," she tells me.

"Really?" I'm not feeling that confident, even though I wish it with all my heart.

"A woman wants to know that she is wanted, even if she currently hates the person wanting her. Just don't be a stalker," she warns. "There's a line between cute and creepy."

Right. Mental note—don't be creepy.

"I've missed you so much, little one," I say, standing up and giving my sister a warm hug.

"That's what family does for one another. Oh, and I saw this bag ..." she says with a giggle.

I shake my head at her. Still missed the little shit. And maybe I do owe her a nice bag for her wise words.

20

LILLY

I've spent the past week crying into my hot cocoa. I know, girl power and all that stuff, but sometimes a girl just wants to wallow in her hot chocolate, bake, and binge-watch *Sex and the City*. I feel bad that I'm more upset over Luca leaving than I ever was about Rob, who's still blowing up my phone, even after I traveled halfway across the world to get away from the bastard.

I don't care for his new year wishes—I don't need them. I'm doing just fine without him.

Oops, I drop some chocolate onto my pajamas and lick it off. *Don't judge. I am fine.*

I'm totally fine.

Honest.

My phone vibrates, and it's another message from Luca. Now, when a girl is at the bottom end of wallowing, she will, you know, cyberstalk the man who broke her heart. And I mean Luca, definitely not Rob.

My heart hurts looking at all his old Instagram photographs. Thankfully, there aren't many of him and his fiancée. The images are mostly of him traveling around the world—casinos in Monaco, private yachts in the south of France, shopping sprees along Rodeo Drive—a whole other life that he led that's so far from the one I live or the person I thought he was.

It's hard meshing Luke and Luca into the one person in my mind, but Luca is persistent, I'll give him that. Even though I haven't responded to a single text message, they still come like clockwork. He tells me about his father, how his health is slowly improving, and how he's finally at home resting. He also texts me messages of how much he misses me and wishes I was by his side during this difficult time. Those messages hurt my heart, and it takes all my willpower not to book a ticket on the next flight to Rome to be with him, especially when he adds in some dirty talking—those sexts really kill my resolve.

But let's face it, a prince and a doctor don't fit the fairy tale mold. Do they?

My phone rings again, and this time it's from a number I don't know.

"Hello."

"Buongiorno. Is this Miss Lilly Simpson?" a happy-sounding Italian man greets me on the phone, and my heart begins to thump wildly in my chest. I wouldn't put it past Luca to find a way for me to take his calls.

"Si," I say cautiously.

"Fantastico. My name is Andrea Rossi. His Highness Principe Luca put me in touch with you." *His Highness—that sounds strangely weird when it's spoken out loud.* "He said you would be perfect for our organization."

"Oh, really." I'm surprised that Luca kept his word.

"I've had a look at your resume, and your experience is exactly what we're looking for … young, passionate people who want to help the world."

"Thank you so much, that's very kind of you to say. What is it exactly that you do?"

"Ah, of course, scusa. I'm the CEO of Italy's largest global charity foundation. We distribute millions of dollars every year to charities around the world. We're looking for doctors with experience on the ground to help us distribute the money and set up more beneficial programs to help the world's underprivileged. Instead of just handing over money, which can fall into the wrong hands, we want to diversify and make sure it's handled correctly."

Wow. This sounds amazing and is exactly what I'd love to do.

"So, I wouldn't necessarily be a doctor on the ground?"

"Not all the time, no, but we'd make sure all your certificates stay current with ongoing learning. You would be on the ground helping set up certain programs. You would also drop in on others to check they are running smoothly from a medical standpoint."

"This sounds very interesting to me," I say.

"It is … and you're perfecto. I'll email you an information pack about our organization as well as the contract and job description. Take your time to peruse, and if you're interested, we'd love to have an interview with you."

This sounds so incredibly unique that I'm excited about the prospect of running this for them. "That sounds perfect. Thank you so much for the opportunity, Mr. Rossi."

"Grazie, Miss Simpson," he says before hanging up.

I do a little dance around the cottage once the phone call ends. Crumbs fall from my chest all over the floor. My mind turns to Luke, sorry Luca, and how I want to call and thank him for the opportunity. He's been persistent but respectful of my need for space.

I miss him.

So much it sucks.

The cottage is quiet without him here.

Stupidly, I haven't even changed the sheets because I can still smell his cologne all over them. I'm a sad, sad woman. Picking up my phone, I stare at the only picture we have together, and I run my fingers over his perfect face.

"Urgh," I moan, throwing it to the side.

Be strong, Lilly.

Remember, you promised yourself this year was all about you being selfish.

But can't I selfishly want someone I can't have?

I've spent enough time being a sad sack, I need to move on and start a fresh, and this job opportunity might be it. So, it's time to get your ass into the shower, freshen up, and go join the land of the living at the pub. So, that's exactly what I do.

* * * *

Nervously, I walk back into the pub. The last time I was here was with Luca for Christmas Eve, which now seems like a lifetime ago. As soon as the door opens, everyone stops to see who's entering the bar. Everyone raises their drinks to me and continues on with what they were doing.

"Lilly." Wallace gives me a big bear hug. "Happy New Year, it's great tae see ye."

"It's good to see you, too," I say while pulling up a bar stool.

"What can I get ye?" he asks.

"Whisky, please."

He nods, then busies himself.

"Where's the hot man ye had wit ye last time?" Donna asks as she takes a seat beside me and smiles.

"He had to go back to Italy. His father had a heart attack," I tell her. Just thinking about Luca makes my heart hurt.

"Oh, no. Will he be back?" she asks, concerned.

Wallace places the glass of whisky in front of me, and I throw it back all in one go. Wallace and Donna look at each other with concern in their eyes.

"Ye know ye can talk to me?" Donna says as she wraps her arm around my shoulders tenderly.

Tears begin to well in my eyes. "Everything is a mess, Donna."

She looks at me with concern. "Another drink, Wallace," she tells her husband.

He silently pours me another glass.

"I know I'm not ye ma, but I have some good ears on me."

This makes me smile through my tears because Donna and Wallace are good people.

So, I start at the beginning.

"Rob was a little shite," Donna seethes.

"I'll knock his block off when he shows his face in town," Wallace says as he slams his hand on the bar making the glasses jiggle.

"So ye have feelin's for the Italian?" Donna asks me.

"Yep."

"But now is nae the right time?"

I nod my head in agreement.

"He seemed like a good man. I think ye should take the charity job," Donna tells me.

"Aye, me, too," Wallace adds.

"We're very proud of ye, Lilly," Donna adds.

Dammit, Donna's hitting me with the feels.

"And ye're family to us," Wallace states.

Fuck it. I let the tears fall down my cheeks. I mean, Wallace has been plowing me with whisky since I arrived, and in the emotional state I have been in, of course, the tears would be flowing soon anyway.

"If Luca's the one, ye will find each other again," Donna suggests.

Maybe Donna's right.

"Thank you," I say, wrapping my arms around her.

"It's all good, lassie. Now let's get ye somethin' to eat to soak up all this whisky," Donna says with a grin.

Sounds like a plan.

21

LUCA

"**M**y love, how are you?" my mother greets me warmly, placing two kisses on each of my cheeks.

"I'm doing okay," I answer.

"You seem sad, my boy?" she says as she takes my hand in hers and sits with me on the sofa.

"How's Papá?" I ask.

"Your father is doing fine. He's cranky over not being able to drink his wine," she states, shaking her head at him.

"I'm sorry I left," I tell her, giving her hand a squeeze.

My mother reaches out and caresses my face. "What happened, my love?"

I've been dreading this question. I knew there'd be a time when we'd have to address it, but I'm not sure how she's going to react.

"I found out Rachele wasn't faithful to me," I tell her softly.

Shock radiates from my mother as her hand flies to cover her mouth. "No. I do not believe it!" she says, shaking her head.

"She and Marcus have been seeing each other for years."

Her eyes widen like saucers as she continues to shake her

head in disbelief. "Rachele comes from a respectable family, son. I don't believe she'd do this to you ... to us."

My stomach sinks at her reaction. But, of course, Allegra and Rachele have been doing damage control, and she is inclined to believe them more than me at this moment.

"I saw them at the rehearsal, Mama ... with my own eyes."

Her brows pull together. I know she wants to believe me, but she can't fathom the person Rachele is in front of her with the Rachele we all get behind closed doors. Someone sent me a video and I never wanted to use it, but I have to take back control of the situation.

"Here, Mama, press play," I state while handing my phone over to her.

She clutches her chest as she watches the video someone took of Rachele and Marcus together. Tears fall down her cheeks as she hands the phone back to me.

"I'm so sorry," she whispers as I pull her into my arms to comfort her.

"It's not your fault, Mama," I tell her.

"Never thought either of them could be capable of this," she says, shaking her head in disbelief. It takes a glass of wine for her to settle her nerves after the revelation.

"Did Allegra know?" she asks me.

I'm not going to lie to cover my sister's ass, not after the stunt she pulled in Edinburgh. "Yes, she'd been the one covering it up over the years."

My mother swears under her breath. "That's why you disappeared?"

I nod in agreement.

"Is it true that you met someone while you were in Scotland?" she asks.

Let me guess, Allegra told her. "Yes, a woman called Lilly. She's a doctor." Just saying her name out loud is an ache in a void that never seems to end.

My mother shifts around in her seat, grimacing, looking guilty suddenly. "A doctor? I was led to believe she was after your money."

"Never. Lilly didn't know who I was until Allegra and Rachele showed up and told her," I explain to my mother.

"I realize now that I have been fooled," she confesses angrily.

"She isn't interested in all this ..." I say as I wave my hand around the opulent surroundings of my family's home. "Otherwise, she would be here with me now, if she did."

My mother falls quiet. "I know. I did a background check on her."

I lean back in shock at her. I would expect this from Allegra, even Giorgio but not my own mother. "You what?"

"I'm sorry, *Luca*. Your sister led me down the wrong path. I was trying to protect you," she tells me apologetically.

"And you found nothing, right?" I ask angrily. I can't believe she did this.

She nods in agreement. "Honestly, I found a truly accomplished woman. There was one thing I didn't understand, though. Why did she leave Africa before her tenure was up? It said she has a fiancé there?"

Guess her file hasn't been updated. "That's her ex. He was cheating on her."

My mother's body relaxes a little at that bit of information.

"She was stuck watching him fool around with the nurses because she was unable to leave until her time was up. Another doctor wanted to stay, so they swapped positions, and she came home. Unfortunately, or fortunately for me, her sister went to Africa to surprise her, so when Lilly arrived home, she found me instead." I leave out the naked part, my mother has no need to know.

"Oh my, that poor girl. Why do people not take their

promises seriously anymore?" my mother states angrily, shaking her head.

"I gave her name to Andrea Rossi …" my mother nods, "… I think she'd be perfect for the charity." I didn't tell Lilly that the charity was my family's. She didn't need to know that, also Andrea would not hire her if she truly couldn't do the job no matter who is paying his wages.

"Yes, she will. Her resume is stellar."

High praise from my mother.

"Do you have feelings for this girl?" she asks hesitantly.

"Yes. I've never felt this way before with anyone," I tell her honestly.

She raises a brow at me in surprise.

"But I don't think it's our time, yet. We both have some baggage to get through."

My mother waves my concerns away. "If you think she is worth the fight, then fight."

"Really?"

"I want you to be happy," she says, placing her hands on either side of my face again. "That's all a mother ever wants. I'm a mother first, a princess second," she tells me.

I wrap my arms around her tightly and give her a big hug.

"I'll not stand in your way, Luca. If she is who you want," she tells me honestly.

"Thank you, Mama," I say, giving her the biggest kiss on the cheek.

I think it's going to take a lot of work to get Lilly back, but I'm up for the challenge.

22

LILLY

"Hello, anyone home," Laura calls out as she enters the cottage.

"You're home," I scream, seeing my sister for the first time in years. We run toward each other, and both of us reach out for the biggest hug. I never want to let her go as I wrap my arms around her. Tears are already falling down my cheeks. "I've missed you so much."

"I've missed you too," she says, hugging me tighter.

"Let me see the ring," I ask, grabbing at her hand.

She shows me her gorgeous sage green sapphire with a gold band inset with diamonds. It is so beautiful and unique just like her.

"I'm so happy for you." I squeal with delight. "And were you happy with the proposal? Was it everything you dreamed of?"

"Never in my mind did I ever think Andy would be proposing to me in Zanzibar. If someone had told me that, I would have laughed. But he did, and it was magical, and I will never forget that moment for the rest of my life," she says, smiling.

"Where is Andy?"

"He went home to check in with his family. See how Nanny Stewart is going. Thank you so much for rescuing her."

I wave her thanks away. "Glad it wasn't serious, and she's all recovered."

"How are you going?" she asks, rubbing my arm.

"Everything is fine. Don't worry about me. Come on, you and I need to catch up," I say, dragging her into the cottage where I start to fix us both a cup of tea so we can snuggle into the couches and chat. Something I haven't been able to do for years.

Once we are all settled into our comfy spots, the fire is at the perfect setting, and the tea is soothing my soul, I can relax.

"Now that you're engaged, does that mean Andy is moving in here or are you moving into Andy's parent's place?" I ask my sister.

"We haven't thought that far yet," she answers as she takes a sip of her tea.

"I'm guessing being a farmer he must be up early with them. And not like the cottage is far from his farm but ..."

"He did mention that he has a block of land on the farm that was always his to build on once he was married, maybe we might do that, but I'm not sure if I want to leave the cottage," Laura explains to me.

"You don't need to make any decisions now, but the cottage is small if you eventually want to have a family."

"Are you planning on staying and living in the cottage?" she asks me.

I shake my head. "Not sure. We'll see how this interview goes with the charity in Rome. I might be moving to Italy, or it could be a bust and you'll be stuck with me forever."

"Glencoe is too small for you, Lilly. You were made to help the world with your gift."

Tears begin to well in my eyes at my sister's compliment.

"Have you heard from Luca?" she asks.

"He keeps texting me. But I haven't replied."

"Lilly!" my sister exclaims.

"I know, I know. I don't know what to say to him. My emotions are all over the place when it comes to him. I'm scared. I don't want to get hurt again. Don't think I could handle it a second time," I confess.

"What is worse, taking a chance or never knowing?" she asks wisely.

I shake my head at her because she is right, and I don't want to hear it right now.

"How are the parentals?"

"Disappointed but that isn't new."

"What about Rob? Heard from that little fucker," she asks, and I can see the venom written across her sapphire blue eyes.

"He's blocked. I sent the ring back. Mom and Dad gave me lectures on how this is going to embarrass them with their friends, but I don't care. This isn't about them. This is about me and what I want out of life."

"Which is Luca, the hot Italian prince," Laura says, chuckling.

"No more men until I've sorted out my life," I tell her.

"Oh, come on, you must have thought about what it would be like to be a princess," Laura teases.

Maybe in a dark moment, I let myself think what it would be like. How much good in the world I could do with that kind of title, but I can't forget all the other stuff that comes with it. I'm a hot mess. I googled Luca one night I was drunk. He's so hot. Images of him dressed in a tuxedo, looking regal AF. Countless magazine articles about his love life and images of him and Rachele together, looking like the perfect couple. There were a couple of articles about the wedding being postponed saying it was because his father had a heart attack, but there was no mention of Rachele's unfaithfulness. Does that mean they are back together? I wouldn't blame him. She's gorgeous and has the right credentials with her family connection to them.

"Don't think I'm princess material," I say, answering her question.

"Only because you have a proper job. Are there any princesses that are doctors? I'm not up with news of Europe's royal families."

"Who knows. Can't imagine you could continue working normally if you're a princess."

"True." Laura nods. "Lucky it didn't work out then," she says, giving me a wry smile.

※ ※ ※ ※

"Good luck today," Laura says as she kisses me goodbye.

I'm off to Rome to meet Mr. Rossi and interview for the position with the charity. It looks fantastic and feels like it's what I need in my life at the moment. Give me purpose and a clean slate.

"I'm going to need it," I say, hugging my sister one last time.

"You're a catch, Lilly. Don't let anyone tell you otherwise. You've got this. I have faith. And if you run into Luca while you are there, just hear him out," she tells me.

My stomach does somersaults at the thought that I might run into Luca while I'm in Rome. I mean, Rome is a big place, it's not likely I'll run into him, is it?

"You think I will?"

"Maybe, be prepared in case you do," she warns me.

She's right. Prepare myself. He did suggest me for this job, so I shouldn't assume I won't see him. He's a prince. Isn't he kind of busy?

"Don't stress, Lilly. Go there. Kick butt and get the job. You deserve it," Laura says, giving me a pep talk.

Think of all the good you can do.

I give my sister one last hug before leaving the cottage.

※ ※ ※ ※

I'm so nervous my leg will not stop bouncing as the car races through the ancient streets of Rome to my hotel. I have an interview with Andrea Rossi, the CEO of the charity foundation today. I run through all the points I want to touch on in the interview and try to mentally prepare myself. As we continue to drive through Rome, my mind wanders to Luca. He said he split his time between Rome, Florence, and Milan. Does that mean he's in Rome now?

Does he know I have the interview today? No, the man is a prince, he's too busy to worry about what I'm doing.

I continue to stare out the window and notice how fashionable and beautiful all the women are walking along the streets. Then look down at my clothes. Didn't have much in the way of interview wear, didn't need it in Africa. I'm lucky that I had some things at the cottage and that they still fit, but I feel utterly inadequate compared to these stylish women.

Then I remember the images I saw of Rachele. Looking gorgeous in head-to-toe designer. How could I ever compete with that? Luca was slumming it with me, the girl from the cottage.

I still don't understand why he keeps messaging me every couple of days, especially since there's been no announcement of his breakup. I will not be the side chick. Even though I do look forward to getting them, which sucks. But it's for the best. If I do get the job, I will send him one then, thanking him for putting me forward, and if I don't, then that's the end of it.

The sleek black Mercedes pulls up out the front of a tall glass office building.

"I'll take your bags to the hotel, Miss Simpson," the driver advises me as he helps me out of the car.

"Grazie."

I take a moment to compose myself and walk into the luxurious building. I check in with the building's receptionist. She hands me a special day pass and gives me directions to the twentieth floor.

Here I go, all or nothing.

I needn't have worried because the interview was a success. They offered the job to me on the spot, and I couldn't say no. I get to help save people's lives with lots and lots of money, and that's difficult to say no to anyway.

My driver is waiting for me out the front of the building and takes me to my hotel. Picking up my phone, I send Luca a text message.

Lilly: *Thank you for introducing me to Mr. Rossi. I got the job.*

My heart is racing as the sound of the text sending echoes through the car. Not long after leaving the office building, my driver is pulling up out the front of a gorgeous old building near the famous Spanish Steps.

"Signora Simpson, welcome," a well-dressed doorman greets me at the door.

This hotel has great customer service.

"Grazie," I say as I follow him into a grand foyer. I notice there isn't a reception desk, which is weird. Perhaps I came in the back entrance or something. He holds open the lift door for me, and I follow, then he hits the 'A' button. Usually, the top button is for the penthouse suite, and attico is the Italian word for penthouse.

This charity has gone all out.

I feel bad because this must have cost them a pretty penny to put me up like this.

"We are here," he says as the lift doors open, and the man asks me to step out.

Which I do, right into a grand marbled foyer. But what gains my attention instantly at the end of the foyer is a terrace, and all I can see are grand Italian buildings all around me. I rush outside and take in the picturesque view. We're right above the Spanish Steps with some other famously old buildings surrounding me, but I have no idea what they are.

"It's beautiful, isn't it?"

That voice.

The one I have missed for the past couple of weeks.

No. He can't be here.

I feel his presence behind me, but I don't dare look.

"Lilly, please look at me," he asks.

No. My hands are shaking, I'm not prepared to see him. I need more time. I take in a deep breath and turn around. Nothing in my head prepares me for the man standing in front of me. This man really is gorgeous. The man, right here, definitely looks like a prince. His scruff has been shaved off and replaced with a clean-cut vibe. His inky black hair is slicked back, and he's dressed in a killer suit.

"You look good," he says. That cocky smirk is still planted on his gorgeous face as chocolate eyes drift over me from head to toe.

My body warms under his intense gaze. "What are you doing here?" I ask angrily.

"I wanted to say congratulations in person on your new job," he says with a shrug.

My eyes narrow—I have only just texted him. He made it here quickly. "Thank you." My eyebrows pull together because something isn't right.

"You'll be an incredible asset to our company," he says.

I still.

Our company.

"This is your charity?" I question him.

Luca realizes his faux pas because the tone of my voice tells him what I think about that.

"My family and I raise a lot of money for that charity. I'm its patron," he explains.

"And you didn't think you should've mentioned this to me?" I ask.

"I thought you would be happy," he says as he looks at me, lines forming in his forehead. Not understanding why I would be upset.

"You tricked me," I tell him angrily.

The room goes silent at my accusation.

"What? No. Lilly, no."

"I can't take the job. This is another lie. Why do you always lie?" I yell at him as I push past and begin to search the enormous penthouse for my bag. "How big is this fucking place?" I yell, opening up a million and one doors.

"It's the door on the end. My bedroom," he states.

I still. My stomach sinks at the revelation that he's just dropped on me.

"This is *your* home?" I ask, looking around at the opulent apartment.

"Si."

"I was told it was a hotel."

"It isn't."

"You lied to me again. Enough with lies. I can't take it anymore," I say, throwing my hands up.

"Lilly?" he calls my name softly, unsure of what he should do because I'm guessing this is not the reaction he thought would be happening.

"Why did you bring me here?"

Luca looks at me, grimaces, then swallows hard. He digs his hands into his pockets. "Because I've missed you, Lilly."

No. He doesn't get to say those things to me.

"I thought that maybe you would love it and want to share it with me."

My heart beats uncontrollably in my chest. He thinks a

gorgeous apartment with a killer view would make me forget everything. *It is sweet.* No, it's not. He lied to me about the job and lied to me again about the apartment. How can I trust him? I reach out to steady myself. Am I having a panic attack?

"Lilly," Luca calls out as he moves toward me, but stops himself from reaching for me.

"I don't belong here," I tell him. My words come out in barely a whisper as I lean back against the wall, letting the cool surface calm me.

"You belong with me?" he tells me. I can see the pleading behind those chocolate eyes.

No. Please don't say those things to me, Luca. I'm trying to be strong.

"No, I don't. You belong to another."

Luca stills as his dark brows pull together as if trying to work out my thought process.

"There's been no mention in the media about you and Rachele splitting," I question him.

Luca nods. "As you know my father was unwell. Both families agreed that we would wait until he was given the all-clear before releasing the news. This morning he was given the all-clear. The press release was sent out an hour ago. Everyone will know that the wedding was canceled due to unfortunate circumstances happening the night before the wedding. I also wanted to make sure everyone knew that Rachele and I have been done since that night three months ago."

Oh.

"Things are about to get crazy for me. The paparazzi will be on high alert once the news begins to circulate, but I'm hoping that it is something you and I can weather together," he states.

"We'd never work."

"Why?" he questions me.

"You're a prince, and I'm a doctor. We come from two

different worlds. All we had in common was a broken heart and being stuck in a cottage during a snowstorm," I tell him.

Luca takes a step back as if my words slapped him.

"I still love you, Lilly," he declares.

Love.

As if love is enough. There is a huge mountain between us. How can we possibly get over it?

"You don't lie to the one you love," I tell him.

Luca's shoulders sink. "I didn't tell you who I was because, for the first time in my life, no one knew. There were no preconceptions of me. I could be me. Not put on this princely facade. I gave you the real me, Lilly. The me that I could never be because of my title."

Tears well in my eyes at his words.

"Did I tell you that the charity was my family's? No. Because I knew you wouldn't go for the job and honestly, we need good doctors on our team. I was thinking more about the people we could save with having you on board than myself," he explains.

Damn him.

"And the lie about this being a hotel and not my home. Okay. I'll take that one. I just needed to see you again. I wanted a chance to see you again. To talk to you. Have you been getting my texts?"

I nod my head.

"Good. I can't apologize enough for everything that happened New Year's Day. That is not at all how I wanted things to end between us. But I understand how shocking that would have been to wake up too. Just know that what my sister did, the family is furious with her over it."

Guess that makes me feel a little bit better.

"I brought you here because I wanted to show you my world. This is me too," he says, waving his hand around the opulent apartment. "And the man you met, naked in a snowed-in cottage is me too."

Can I love those two men, or can I only love the one in the cottage?

"I've missed you," he confesses.

Tears threaten to fall. "I've missed you, too," I confess. Because I do. Seeing him in front of me, everything I felt for him for those couple of weeks comes flooding back.

Luca moves closer, his body is inches away from mine, the heat radiating off him. I open my eyes and watch as he takes off his suit jacket, then his tie, throwing them to the ground. He yanks off his cufflinks, and they bounce across the floor. He rolls the cuffs of his business shirt up over his gorgeous olive skin and places his hands on either side of my head. "You can run and run, but … I'll always find you. You're not ready for me yet, I can understand that. I will wait."

His eyes are so serious as he stares at me. "I'll wait until the time comes when you realize that there's no one else in this world who means more to me than you do. I'll wait until you know that I'm loyal and true to only you. I will wait until you realize we do belong together, and that no one will love you with all of their heart more than I do."

Crap on a cracker. That's the sweetest thing anyone has ever said to me.

The tears stream down my cheeks. How the hell is a girl meant to say no to that? Ugh, he's playing dirty.

Fuck it. I lean forward and kiss him.

He's shocked for a mere couple of seconds, but then my Luke is back, pressing me up against the wall, his thick fingers running through my hair, his large palm holding my face as his plump lips kiss me, then his teeth are nipping me. Groans and sighs come from the both of us as tongues collide in a frantic kiss that has built up from these weeks apart.

"Fuck, I've missed you, Lilly."

"Hmmm," I moan as he lifts my pencil skirt, the material

pooling around my waist. "Do you have any idea what I have done to my hand since we've been apart?"

I shake my head as my fingers unbuckle his belt as quickly as I can.

"Blisters, I have given myself blisters from thinking about you. My fucking hand is the poorest substitute for your pussy."

Oh, shit, Luca's brought out the dirty talking already. Yes, Luca, yes.

As I push his suit pants and briefs to the floor, he says, "I need to be inside you, Lilly."

I nod, giving him the green light to do all the dirty, delicious things he wants to do to me.

Luca rips off my panties. Another pair that seemed pretty sturdy, but against his hands, just tear to shreds. He's lifting one of my legs and hooking it around his waist as he enters me in one easy thrust.

"Merda, *Shit,*" he hisses, burying himself inside of me.

I feel so full. Has he always been this big? My fingers dig into his fleshy globes, urging him on more, needing him, needing us. My back rubs against the wall. The painting further down shakes as he frantically thrusts into me. *Yes, yes, yes.*

If this is what fate had in mind, then I believe.

I'm a believer.

"You're never running again, Lilly. Do you hear me?"

I mumble something incoherent because I'll say yes to pretty much anything right at this moment if he continues to fuck me like he is.

"It's you and me."

"Yes. Oh, yes." I scream as we both tumble over the edge together.

"That was …" Both of us are breathing heavily.

"Unexpected," he finishes my sentence and grins while tucking himself back into his trousers.

"Yes, unexpected," I agree. Pulling my pencil skirt down.

I'm going to have to go commando because he's ripped my panties to shreds. *Again.*

"I've missed you so much." Luca reaches for me, but I move out of his way. Hurt falls across his face. "Lilly?"

Shaking my head.

"I thought …?" he questions, looking between us.

He thought a quickie in his apartment was going to solve everything that has happened between us. Like I said before, there is a mountain between us and it's one that isn't so easy to climb over.

"That was physical. Something we both couldn't stop. But I need to stop this now," I tell him honestly.

Luca is surprised.

"I appreciate your help, Luca, but I made it clear that I was done being pushed around for the benefit of others. My family and Rob used me for their own agenda. And I've had enough of it," I tell him.

"You think I'm using you for an agenda?" he asks, confused.

"In your own way, yes. You pushed me into the job at your charity. Yes, it is a dream job, and I can't thank you enough for putting my name up for it, but the charity is still linked to you. Then pretending this apartment was a hotel so that you could see me again."

"You weren't returning my texts. There was no other way to see you," I exclaim.

"And that was for a reason," I argue back.

"Because you're stubborn and afraid of what I am offering you," he bites back.

"You're offering me what? A life of opulence, a microscope on every little thing that I do, making me give up medicine? Not every little girl grows up to want to be a princess, Luca," I tell him.

"I thought I was offering you my heart. All the other stuff means nothing to me. It's all just stuff," he says sadly.

Oh. I feel like a bitch now. But it is my truth. It's how I feel. He's asking me to be something I'm not. I'm not sophisticated nor elegant enough to be a princess. I would only be letting him and his family down.

"Medicine takes up a huge portion of my heart, Luca. Partners have always come second to my true love which is medicine. I don't want to lie to you, Luca. It's taking up more of my heart than I can give you. And you deserve someone that can give you their whole heart, not the bits left over that aren't broken."

Luca's face falls at my words. I hate doing this to him. But it's for the best, my heart hurts enough. If we continue any further my heart will never recover from Luca Fiorenzo.

"I promised myself I was going to be selfish this year, Luca. After everything I went through last year. I sat in silence for too long biting my tongue, doing something I wasn't happy doing for the sake of not rocking the boat," I explain as I nervously play with my bracelet. "The hardest thing I've ever had to do is stand here and tell you these things, especially after what just happened."

He sags against the wall, defeat written all over his face. "You may have feelings for me, but it's not enough, is that right?" he questions me.

I nod.

"What you mean is, I'm not enough."

Shaking my head, that isn't at all what I mean. Walking over, I stand in front of him.

"You are enough," I say, reaching out and cupping his face. "I wish I'd met you at a different time in my life not when it wasn't such a dumpster fire. As much as what we had together in the cottage helped me, it didn't heal me. You showed me that I deserved so much more than Rob ever gave me and I can't thank you enough for that. But I need to find me, Luca. I've had to suppress Lilly Simpson for the past couple of years while away.

The once happy-go-lucky woman I was before I left for Africa has shriveled up into a woman who has trust issues and numerous other titles of baggage. I don't think I could love you in the way that you deserve, not right now. I don't love me in the way I deserve either. And I want to. I need to," I explain. I hope that makes sense.

"I get it, Lilly. I don't like it or want it, but I get it," he says sadly.

"I really am sorry, Luca."

He simply shakes his head.

There isn't anything else left to say. I turn on my heel and head toward the bedroom to grab my things. As I walk away, they are some of the most painfully slow steps I have ever walked in my life.

23

LILLY

Déjà vu. Here I am in my cottage crying into my duvet over a man. It was the hardest thing in the world to walk away from Luca in that moment. I know I broke his heart. It broke my heart too.

"It was the right thing to do," Laura says as she cuddles me in bed.

"My heart hurts so much," I tell her.

"I know, but it wasn't the right time for you both," she says, stroking my hair.

"What happens if he moves on?" I cry.

Laura frowns. "He might. He's a single man. A prince. He's not going to stay single forever."

That isn't what I want to hear as I break down further.

"I'm sorry. I didn't mean to upset you. Thought I was help-ing. You will move on too. You don't know who is around the corner."

I don't want anyone else. *But you rejected him.* I know I did. And I understand all the reasons I had to. And I think Luca did too. Still doesn't mean that I can't have a breakdown about it.

Luca hasn't messaged me once since I've come back from Rome. He's done with me.

※ ※ ※ ※

"Are you going to be okay?" Laura asks me as Andy grabs her bags from the hallway and takes them to the car.

"Yes. I'm fine. Go. Have fun. Enjoy London. Say hi to Mom and Dad for me," I tell her. Laura is off to her high school reunion this weekend down in London. And while she is there Mom and Dad want to catch up and celebrate her engagement.

"I'm worried. It's been a week, and you haven't gotten out of bed," she says, narrowing her eyes at me.

"I promise I'll be fine. I have all my stuff that's arrived from Africa. And then I've got to get things ready to move to Rome. It's going to be a weekend of getting myself sorted," I tell her.

"I'm worried seeing all the things from Africa is going to spiral you," Laura states cautiously.

Reaching out, I pull my sister into a hug, letting her know 'thank you for your concern, but it's going to be okay'. "It's fine. That's what the whisky is for. To help delete the memories," I joke.

Laura looks concerned.

"Andy, please take your fiancée. I'm fine. Have fun," I tell my sister. Andy is pulling her away from the entrance of the cottage as I wave her goodbye. She gives me a weak wave, and I know she is upset, but she's only trying to look after me.

There's a knock at my door. Laura and Andy have only been gone thirty minutes, I hope they haven't forgotten anything. I head toward the door and open it. Genuinely thinking I will see my sister's pissed-off face, upset she forgot something.

I freeze.

My eyes blink a couple of times not believing what I am

seeing. This must be a nightmare. There is no way in hell he is standing there before me.

"It's been a while, Lilly," Rob states, giving me a smile.

Is he serious? What the hell?

"It's freezing out here, Lil. Can I come in?" he asks as if we are old friends.

Who the hell does he think he is?

There are fluffy white flecks swirling around him. He can freeze to death for all I fucking care.

"Please, we need to talk," he asks.

There's nothing to talk about. Literally nothing. But unfortunately, I think what my gran would say to be leaving someone on the cottage's front step in the snow. She would be disappointed, no matter who they were that I would do that to someone in their time of need.

"Fine," I grumble, opening the door further for him.

He steps inside and shakes off the frozen flecks, then shucks off his coat and hangs it up like he has done a million times before.

"Don't get too comfortable. You won't be staying long," I say before ushering him into the living room where he can warm up by the fire. Hurt falls across his face at my barb, which surprises me. "Would you like a tea or coffee?" I ask him.

"Coffee, please," he answers as he warms his hands in front of the fireplace.

I busy myself in the kitchen, grabbing a mug out of the cupboard and heaping a couple of spoonful's of instant coffee into it. A memory flutters through my subconscious remembering how much Luca hates instant coffee. This makes me smile.

"What are you smiling at?" Rob asks.

His voice catches me off-guard, and I shake the thoughts of Luca from my mind.

"I knew you'd be happy to see me," he says as he wraps his arms around me and pulls me to his chest.

"Get off me," I say, pushing out of his embrace. "What the hell do you think you are doing?" I scream at him.

Rob jumps back and stares at me in shock. "I was trying to hug my fiancée."

"I'm not your fiancée, Rob. What the hell? I'm not happy to see you," I tell him forcefully.

"You're not?"

Has this man got amnesia or something? Why the hell would I be happy to see that cheating bastard?

The whistle of the kettle grabs my attention, and I pick it off its stand and pour the hot water into the mug, then grab the milk.

"But you still remember how I like my coffee," he states.

Huh? Looking down at the coffee, I realize out of habit I've made him his coffee the exact way he likes it. What the hell was I thinking? I wasn't. I'm in shock seeing my ex in my kitchen, when I thought he was halfway across the world. Me remembering how to make his coffee is not a sign that I'm still in love with him. Is he delusional? *Obviously, he is here in Glencoe.*

"It's just coffee. Nothing more, don't read into it. Why are you here, Rob?" I ask, placing the mug of coffee in front of him.

He takes the mug and holds it between his hands. "I think we need to talk."

"No, we don't. I've said everything I need to say to you," I tell him as I cross my arms over my chest.

"Please, Lilly."

My eyes narrow on him, but I will say I am curious he has come a long way to talk to me. Does he not live there anymore? Has he quit?

"I have one week's leave," he adds, reading my thoughts. "Your parents pulled some strings." *Ah, of course, they did.*

"And where are you going for that?" I ask because there is no way in hell it's with me.

"Um ..." he says, his green eyes widening as he looks around the room.

"No way in this world," I yell as I slam my hand down on the counter. "You can get on the next plane to who knows where, but you're *not* staying here."

"Lilly Pilly. We need to work out this misunderstanding," he coos, using his horrible nickname for me which makes my skin crawl.

Work out this misunderstanding? There was no misunderstanding. I understood quite well he's a cheating asshole.

"You fucked every single available woman at our camp. Where is the misunderstanding in that?" I question. *Is this man a complete moron?*

"And yet, you had someone in your bed not that long ago," he says, nodding his head in the direction of my bedroom.

After we broke up. I remember his phone call when Luca ripped him a new one.

"I'm single, Rob. I can do what I want," I explain to him as I cross my arms again. "Unlike you who was messing about on your fiancée right in front of her eyes."

Rob puts his mug of coffee down. "It was just sex, Lilly. What don't you get?"

Fuck him. "Then, why don't you go back out that door and *just have sex* all you like out there?" I point to the front door.

"Because you'll make a good wife," he argues.

What in the actual hell? "You want a shiny trophy wife on your arm. Is that what you want, Rob?"

The bastard has the audacity to roll his eyes at me.

"What has gotten into you, Lilly? You were never this combative," he grumbles.

Because you wore me down, asshole, with all your cheating. "I finally grew some balls, and I'm sticking up for myself."

His lip curls up at my words. "You know this ..." he waves

his hands in the air, "... is very undignified. Your parents would be most upset."

What an asshole bringing my parents into this fight. Even if his words are true. "Hear me and hear me good ... I do *not* give a single fuck."

Watching Rob's face pale at my words gives me butterflies, something he's never been able to produce before.

My phone starts ringing which cuts the tension in the kitchen. I round the kitchen counter and frantically look for my phone. I can hear it but can't see where the hell it is as the ringing tone echoes through the small cottage space. Then I remember it was in my hand when I answered the front door, and I must have dropped it. Leaving Rob in the kitchen, I race to the front door and stare down at the ringing phone.

'Luca' flashes across the screen.

What in the hell is happening? Fate. What the hell gives, girl? You trying to kill me here? The phone eventually rings out, and I let out a heavy sigh. I bend down and pick up the cell and place it back into my pocket.

I need to deal with the dickhead in my kitchen before I can deal with Luca.

"Rob," I call out to my former fiancé as I walk back into the kitchen. He's standing there sipping his coffee as if he doesn't have a care in the world. I wonder what the hell I ever saw in him. I mean, he's not ugly with his blond hair, sparkling green eyes, his height, he looks after himself, and he's a doctor. Let's face it, he'd be a catch for most women just not for me.

He turns around, and I see hope flash across his face as I walk back into the kitchen.

"Can we have a proper talk? Cut out all the other bullshit," I ask as I point to the two armchairs in the living room.

He picks up his mug of coffee and joins me there.

"Were you ever happy with me?" I ask.

"Of course—"

I cut him off because I can see the bullshit ready to flow from his mouth. "Be honest, Rob. Please?"

He lets out a heavy sigh. "No."

Praise be, he is finally being truthful.

"It's not that I didn't like you. You're a beautiful and accomplished woman."

Was not expecting a compliment from him.

"You just didn't love me?" I ask him.

Silence fills the room as Rob works out how to answer that question. Eventually, he ends up shaking his head. "I liked you, and I thought our love would grow over time. Like it did with our parents."

Guess neither one of us had the most loving parents growing up so didn't know what real love was.

"Why did you never talk to me? Tell me any of this?" I ask him.

"You were already in love with me. I didn't want to rock the boat," he says with a shrug.

Maybe there was some truth in that. I genuinely thought I was in love with him, but I'm thinking maybe I was forcing myself to be in love with him because that's what I thought I had to do.

"Instead, you chose to sleep around with everyone and make a fool out of me?" I ask as my anger bubbles to the surface.

"Not on purpose," he says as he stares intensely into his mug of coffee and sighs.

"Then why?" I ask. Because there is no excuse for the way he treated me.

"Because I wasn't sexually attracted to you," he tells me honestly.

Fuck.

That was a sucker punch to the stomach I wasn't expecting. Tears begin to well in my eyes, but I somehow hold it together.

"Yet, you constantly tried to have sex with me?" I argue

with him.

"I'm a male, and you are beautiful," he says with a shrug of his shoulders as if that reply answers everything.

"You do realize you never made me come, not once when we were together," I yell at him. Low blow but one I needed to get in.

His eyes widen at my insult.

"That once you were finished, I'd always have to finish myself off."

Rob steels himself against my words. "I doubt I never ever gave you an orgasm. I never had any complaints from anyone else," he bites back.

Damn, that was savage, Rob.

"Some women are good at faking it."

Rob's eyes narrow in on me while his cheeks turn red. "Then why did they come back for seconds and thirds."

"Maybe they ran out of batteries in their vibrators."

"Or maybe it was because I wanted to fuck them."

The room falls silent at his insults.

"Lilly ..."

Tears well in my eyes, and the first one falls down my cheek.

"I ..." he stutters.

Shaking my head, I get up and walk out of the living room. That man out there isn't going to get the satisfaction of seeing me cry. Walking into my bathroom, I slam the door shut.

Fuck him!

Letting the tears fall fast now, I know I made the right decision walking away from him in Africa. If my family can't see that, then screw them all. I'd rather be alone.

Collecting myself, I walk back out into the living room where Rob is playing with my phone which must have fallen out when I was on the sofa.

"What are you doing?" I question him.

"Checking the time." My eyes narrow in on him. "Lilly, I'm

sorry. I didn't mean to say those things to you. You bruised my ego."

As if that is an excuse.

"You and me ... we should never have gotten together. We're not right for each other," I tell him.

Rob nods in agreement.

"Our families pushed us together, but they don't care that we aren't the right fit, they just care about how they look to their friends."

His head sags. "But they are still our parents," he argues.

"Yeah, and it's my life."

He nods in agreement. I think he understands now there's no chance between us.

"What do we tell them?" he asks. He looks so confused at the prospect of telling his parents that we aren't together.

Not my problem. "Tell them whatever you want, Rob. I think it's best you leave."

"For what it's worth ..." Rob stands and walks over to me. "I do think you're a pretty special woman. I wish you all the best, Lilly." He leans in to kiss me on the cheek, then heads out the door, grabbing his jacket on the way. He gives me a sad wave and disappears into the night.

Grabbing my phone, I dial Luca. I need to tell him I've made a gigantic mistake. I shouldn't have let fear guide my decisions. He is a good man and a man who loves me. I've been a complete fool.

"The number you are calling is currently unavailable," the telephone voice tells me.

Huh?

I keep trying all night and then again in the morning.

Nothing.

I decide to send him an email instead, and it bounces back.

Luca has blocked me.

Fuck!

24

LUCA

My phone beeps and a message from Lilly pops up.

> Lilly: Please stop calling me. You were nothing more than a holiday fling.

Lilly's words stab me in the heart. I try to call her, but she hangs up on me.

> Lilly: If you don't stop harassing me, I will get a restraining order.

Wait! What?

I let the phone fall from my fingers. What just happened? Does she really mean it?

"I've brought ice cream and *The Notebook* to help you get through your heartbreak." Natalia walks in, takes one look at me, and stills. "What happened?"

"Lilly and I are well and truly over. She said if I don't stop calling her, she will get a restraining order on me."

Natalie's eyes widen in surprise. "No, I don't believe it."

Picking up my phone, I hand it to my sister, and she reads Lilly's text messages.

"Oh, Luca, I'm so sorry. I thought she was special."

"So did I." I sigh. Then my anger over the whole situation bubbles to the surface. "Fuck this! I'm not going to stay home and wallow over a woman who doesn't want me. Let's go out."

The paparazzi have been crazy since the announcement of my split with Rachele. A week later, Rachele and Marcus announce their engagement. To be fair, that was shocking. But good for them, it must be love for them to blow everything up like they did.

"Luca, are you sure?" my sister questions me.

"I'm done hiding away. Everyone else seems to have moved on with their lives except me. I'm done pining away for something that I never had. I'm done. Single, Luca is back," I tell my sister.

"Look, I'm all for blowing off steam, brother, but—"

"No buts, Natalia. I'm going to go out tonight, and I'm going to have some fun with or without you," I tell her.

"Fine, someone has to look after you when you're determined to blow everything up," she says with a roll of her eyes.

※ ※ ※ ※

My head hurts. I think I'm going to be sick.

Why did Natalia let me party so hard last night?

Why is my arm dead?

I try to move it, but it doesn't budge.

What the? Cracking my eyes open, I see red hair fanned out across my arm. My heart rate accelerates dramatically. *Who the hell is this?* She rolls over, and an unfamiliar face comes into view as well as a naked breast.

Shit!

Pulling my arm out from underneath the stranger quietly and

carefully, I jump out of bed hoping not to wake her, and head to the bathroom.

What the hell did I do last night?

The hot water slides over my aching body as the night's events come back into my mind slowly.

Lots to drink.

Partying with my friends.

Loads of beautiful women in the VIP section.

Images of lips on mine.

The feeling of being invincible running through my body.

Clothes being shed.

Pushing her warm body up against a wall.

My head hangs in shame. Why?

A hand comes to rest on my shoulder pulling me from my thoughts, and it makes me flinch. The gorgeous redhead is now naked and in the shower with me.

"You ready for round two, big boy." My dick deflates instantly.

"I'm sorry. I … I think you should go."

Her face drops. "Are you sure?" She attempts to reach for my dick, but I stop her.

"Yes."

"Fine. It was fun. Call me if you're ever in the mood again." She exits the shower in a flurry of excitement and leaves.

Like hell, I'm going to call her.

What the hell have you done, Luca?

Walking out of my bedroom dressed for the day, I find my brother sitting in my lounge room sipping on his espresso.

"There's one on the table for you. Thought you might need one after last night." He smirks, raising a brow at me.

"Thanks." I groan as I take a seat and savor the first sip. This is exactly what I needed to make me feel human again.

"Cute girl," he remarks.

Internally, I groan at his observation.

"Don't want to talk about it. Why are you here?" I ask him.

"Came to see after your stunt last night if you were still interested in employing Lilly Simpson?"

Hearing her name makes my heart ache and not in a good way. If I'm honest, I feel so much guilt about hooking up with someone last night, but Lilly has made it perfectly clear on multiple occasions she doesn't want to be with me. So, I shouldn't feel guilty at all.

"What? Yes, of course. Why wouldn't I?" I ask him.

"Because she broke your heart, brother," Giorgio states as he raises his brow at me.

"I'm adult enough to know she's a brilliant doctor, and having her expertise working with the charity will be beneficial to the underprivileged," I explain to him.

"Noble." My brother smirks at me.

"I'll get over it."

"Seems like you did last night," he says with a chuckle.

Dick.

"We can send her to the other side of the world if that helps. She'd still be helping, but you wouldn't be reminded of the woman who broke your heart," Giorgio suggests.

I balk at his idea at first. I thought Lilly being in Rome was the right thing, but judging by her text messages maybe being in the same city isn't a good idea. Maybe I should look at another location that needs people.

"As long as it's somewhere safe," I tell my brother.

"I'll make sure she is safe, brother." Giorgio nods, and with that, he leaves me to it.

Why do I feel like an asshole for sending her away?

25

LILLY

I t took me a while to come to terms with the fact that Luca has blocked me on everything. Thankfully, not Google, but from what I saw on there, I wish I was blocked there too. There are recent images of him on nights out with his friends with gorgeous women hanging off his arm. He looks like he's having the time of his life.

Maybe it's for the best.

The rose-colored glasses of our relationship seem to have fallen off, and I guess we weren't meant to be. I mean, he's a prince, and I'm a doctor. We could never work in the real world. I'd probably pick up the wrong fork and embarrass him with my inadequacies.

"I can't believe you're leaving already. I feel like I've just got my sister back," Laura says as she cuddles me.

When Laura got home, and I told her that Rob had paid me a visit she went nuclear. She couldn't believe the balls on that man to come to our home and try to win me back. I still don't understand what he was thinking because, in the end, he didn't like me. *His family probably forced him, threatened to take him out of the will.* Only explanation I can think of.

I then told her that while Rob was here, Luca called. I couldn't answer the phone, and by the time I got to call him back, he had blocked me on everything. Laura thought that was strange as did I. Why did he call to then block me? We did some investigating and found the images of him going out and enjoying his single life. Laura curses him all manner of names, but I remind her, he told me he loved me, and he gave me chance after chance to be with him. To take the risk on me. He gave me his heart, and I didn't choose him. I can't be mad. This was my choice. I did this to myself, and I must live with the consequences.

I've just got back from a couple of weeks of training with the charity in Rome and this time I was not given the royal treatment, but the normal person treatment. I never saw Luca around Rome, but I heard the stories, the gossip, every day in the papers. Honestly, I am thankful that when they gave me my placement it wasn't in Italy. I don't think I would be able to cope seeing Luca's love life thrown into my face day in, day out.

I was able to get back to Glencoe for the week before I start my new life in Bangladesh. It wasn't on my list of places to live, but I'm so excited to be heading somewhere that's different from my current life. I'm ready to dive into the rich culture and be totally out of my comfort zone. I want to work in a place that really needs me, and from what Andrea has said they need me there.

"I know. But this is such a great opportunity. Now that Andy loves traveling so much, maybe you can come out and see me," I tell her.

Laura pinches her lips together. "Maybe." She sighs. "Why couldn't they have transferred you to like Wales or something? Least it's closer."

This makes me laugh. "They don't need my help there, not like the people of Bangladesh."

"I know," she says sadly before wrapping her arms around

me again. "I feel like I've just gotten you back, and now you're leaving again."

"It's only a three-month contract. And then who knows? I might be somewhere closer next time," I tell her.

"I hope so. Can you put your name down for something at least in Europe? I could convince Andy to go there. I don't think he wants to do another twenty-hour flight anytime soon."

"I promise, I'll try for somewhere a little closer," I tell her.

"I don't want to say goodbye." Laura sobs.

"Me, either," I say, sobbing too.

"You have to get going, Lilly. Otherwise, you're going to miss your flight," Andy reminds me.

The charity has organized for a driver to take me to the airport which is nice of them. When I step out of the cottage the whole town is outside, clapping and waving Bangladeshi flags. I burst into tears. I wasn't expecting this.

"We are so proud of you," Donna says, giving me a cuddle.

"You've got this, Lassie," Wallace says.

Andy has loaded up my things into the back of the car, and I take one last look at everyone as I get in. I know this is the right move for me, but seeing all this love is making it hard to leave.

※ ※ ※ ※

Three Months Later

Bangladesh—what an amazing experience. The sights and sounds, even the smells, have seeped into my bones in such a short time. I really loved it.

What I realized during my time here is where I want to specialize. I want more to do with women's health and especially human trafficking. I was really exposed to that seedy underground world while in Bangladesh. Refugees are being taken advantage of because they don't have any papers, so therefore,

they don't have a voice. Women who think they are being
employed in domestic service but end up in prostitution. And, of
course, birth control is non-existent in these underdeveloped
nations.

Now my contract is up, I've asked if they would consider
transferring me somewhere where I'll be able to help vulnerable
women. And that's how I find myself in Brindisi, in Southern
Italy. It's a large port town in the Mediterranean. It's also a major
portal for human trafficking because of its proximity to Albania,
which is the gateway to Eastern Europe where most of the girls
come from.

I'm excited to be closer to home for the next six months, but
the reminder that I am in Luca's world hits me again as I see his
face staring at me on every newsstand. I hope being far enough
away from Rome that the gossip of his life will not be as intense
outside of the city.

26

LILLY

Two Months Later

"Oh my god, the prince is coming," Bernadette says as she grabs me, shaking me with excitement.

"Who?" I ask, distracted by the report I'm writing up for my department head.

"Prince Luca. That man is so delicious," she says dreamily.

My stomach sinks right out of me.

Luca? Luca is coming here.

"When?" I ask her, hoping the panic I am feeling doesn't come through in my voice.

"He's here now. You must come and see for yourself. The prince is literally the most gorgeous man in the entire world," she says, going on and on about him.

I can see it on her face how excited she is to meet Luca. I don't need to know how good-looking he is, how delicious he smells, or the way he fills out his expensive suits because I have been trying to forget but failing miserably.

"I must finish this. I'll be out in five," I tell her, hoping she forgets all about me in her mad dash to meet the prince. And I can stay here and not have to meet him.

Bernadette rolls her eyes but runs out the door.

I don't want to see him.

He has made it abundantly clear he wants nothing to do with me, so I'll give him his wish and hide away out here.

"There she is," my boss, Ronaldo, states from behind me. "Our best doctor in the clinic, Lilly Simpson. She's been the biggest godsend. She'll be sadly missed when she leaves us next week to work in Albania."

I can hear the warmth in Ronaldo's voice, and it's nice to know how much I'm appreciated.

Turning around in my chair, I pause when I see who he's talking to.

Shit.

I thought time apart would turn him into something unappealing. Unfortunately, it looks like time has made him even more handsome if that's even possible.

"Lilly, this is His Royal Highness Luca Fiorenzo," Ronaldo announces proudly.

Standing, I bow my head ever so slightly. "It's a pleasure to meet you, Your Highness." Not entirely sure what the protocol is here, so I go for what I've learned watching The Crown. Those chocolate eyes turn almost black as they stare at me. His clean-shaven square jaw is tense—actually, his whole body seems awfully tense—and the silence between us turns more and more awkward.

"May I talk to Miss Simpson for a moment," Luca asks sternly, which surprises my boss.

Please say no. I do not want to be locked in this small space with him.

"Oh, yes, of course. I'll just be outside." My boss's eyes widen at me, wondering why on earth the prince wants to talk to me alone.

Great, now people are going to have questions. Bernadette is never going to stop questioning me about it, either.

Once he's gone, I sit in my chair and return to what I'm doing on the computer, ignoring Luca. I can feel his rage radiating off him from behind me. *Well, screw him,* I say.

"Are you going to get a restraining order on me now that we are this close?" he questions me.

What on earth is he talking about? And why is he so angry with me? He's the one who's been sleeping with every model across Europe. I start hitting random keys on my keyboard with no idea what I'm actually doing. My mind is trying not to focus on the angry man behind me.

"You have nothing to say for yourself?" he questions me.

"Me?" I ask as I swivel my chair around to look at him.

Luca's face looks like thunder, his nostrils are flaring, and his feet are planted wide apart—he could not look any angrier if he tried.

"There's nothing to say. And I'm surprised you think there is since you blocked me from your life, out of the blue."

Those dark chocolate eyes narrow in on me. "Out of the blue?" He looks confused by my statement as his head flicks back. "You're the one who messaged and told me you would call the police if I ever contacted you again."

Wait! What?

"Are you high?" I ask.

"No, I'm not high. Are you?" he asks as he leans forward glaring at me.

"How dare you come in here and accuse me of such a thing?" I say, poking him in his chest. His hard chest. One that I remember licking all over one morning, okay, most mornings. He seems to have been working out, as his chest is even harder than I remember. "Why the hell would I tell you I'd call the police if you ever contacted me again? I tried to call you back when I missed your call ..." I trail off while shaking my head, the reason why doesn't matter right now. "Never mind now, it doesn't matter the reason why I was calling, you blocked me. I got the hint, Luca. I've stayed away. I don't care that you're sleeping with half of Europe."

"I'm single, Lilly. I can do what I damn well want," he snaps back.

"Okay. Run along then. Not sure why you are still standing here talking to me," I bite back.

I hate the way that we are talking to each other. Never thought this is where we would be.

"I'll go as soon as you tell me why the hell you sent me those messages. I don't understand why you hated me so much when all I tried to do was love you," he asks again.

Huh. "What messages? I don't understand what you are talking about?"

He pulls out his phone and plays with it for a bit and then hands it over to me.

Our hands touch, and we both feel the zap. Quickly, we move our hands away from each other.

Looking down at the last text message I sent him, I read it.

> Lilly: Please stop calling me. You were nothing more than a holiday fling.

Then, there was a phone call from Luca.

> Lilly: If you don't stop harassing me, I will get a restraining order.

What in the hell?

"I didn't send you this," I tell him, shaking my head in disbelief.

"Evidence says otherwise, *Lilly*."

The way he says my name, it's with pure disgust. "When did I supposedly send this?"

"The date's there ..." he says as he points to his phone.

I scroll up a little and look at the date.

No.

He ...

No, he wouldn't be that cruel, surely?

Realization sets in.

"That motherfucking little bastard," I curse, handing back the phone to him. I begin pacing the room. I want to punch something. I'm so angry. My hand clutches my chest as it starts to tighten.

Fucking. Fuck.

I can't breathe.

I can't damn well breathe.

"Lilly. Lilly ... are you okay?" Luca asks me as he stares at me in panic.

I start shaking my head rapidly. "I ..." I'm pulling in shallow rapid breaths, "... can't ..." more hyperventilation, "... breathe."

My eyes widen as the panic attack takes over my entire body.

You need to calm down, Lilly.

Calm the fuck down.

"Here ..." Luca says as he grabs a paper bag and places it over my mouth.

I breathe a couple of times, then sit on my seat and slump forward.

Luca crouches between my legs. "Are you okay now?"

Shaking my head, I take a deep breath in, then out, and repeat it a few times to calm myself.

It takes me a full ten minutes to get myself under control.

"I'm sorry," I say, looking up at him.

"What happened? What upset you so much that you had a panic attack?" he asks as he stares up at me from where he is kneeling on the ground.

"The night that message was sent, Rob showed up at my door," I tell him quietly, my throat still too sore to speak.

Luca looks taken aback. His hand reaches out and grips the

arm of my chair tightly, and I notice his knuckles turning white as he grips the arm.

"Are you two back together?" he asks.

I shake my head. "Hell, no. He said some hurtful things that night he visited, and I ended up in tears in my bathroom. When I came out, he was on my phone."

Luca's eyes widen, and realization begins to set in.

"When I questioned him, he said he was looking at the time. I didn't think anything of it until now."

Luca lets out a slew of Italian curse words.

"After Rob left. I called you. His visit made me realize ...." I say, but it doesn't matter anymore. There's too much water under the bridge to go back. A tear slips down my cheek realizing fate fucked me over, again.

"You realized what?" Luca asks, his dark brows pulled together in a frown.

"It's too late now. It doesn't matter," I tell him as another tear falls down my cheek.

"What do you mean it doesn't matter? Of course, it matters. Tell me ..." Luca asks as he reaches out and wipes the tear away from my cheek with his thumb.

I shake my head. We hurt each other too many times to come back from it all. "It won't change anything."

"You don't know that," he says almost on a whisper as he stands.

"Are you happy, Luca?" I ask him.

"I don't know," he says as he rakes his hand through his hair, and his head shakes slowly.

"Before today ... were you happy?"

"I thought I was, but ..."

Shaking my head, I tell him, "I'll never regret our time together, Luca."

"Lilly ..." he says my name. I see the pain etched across his features.

"My life is here helping people ... your life is over there 'helping' people," I tell him.

The door to the room opens and in walks a beautiful younger woman. She looks familiar with her long black hair and chocolate eyes. "We have to go," she says.

Those chocolate eyes are jumping between the two of us, and they are full of concern.

"I hope that has cleared things up, Your Highness," I say to him. Trying to be professional even though I know I look anything but.

Luca looks at me, and I notice the anguish behind his eyes. He wants to say something but now is not the time.

"Luca, we have to go." The woman's a little more forceful this time.

Luca turns on his heels and rushes out the door.

27

LUCA

"That looked intense," Natalia states as we get into the car. We took the helicopter to Brindisi from Rome, and we are on our way back there now. "Are you okay after seeing her again?"

"Fuck," I curse as I tug the ends of my hair with my fingers.

Lilly didn't message me. Rob did. Her damn ex. While she was crying because he said something to upset her.

Fuck.

I should've been there. I should have protected her from him like I promised her I would.

That little fucker. He fucked with what Lilly and I had. He couldn't cope with the fact she didn't want him, that she wanted someone else, so he made it look like she didn't want me anymore, not knowing that would be the final nail in the coffin for us both.

"Fuck," I curse again, punching the seat in front of me.

"Luca!" Natalia screams, her eyes widening at my angry outburst.

"Lilly didn't send the messages, Nat," I tell her.

My sister shakes her head, a little confused over my train of thought. "What messages?"

"The one about the restraining order."

Her eyes widen remembering the story. "Who … who sent it, then?"

"Her ex was there the night they were sent to me. That's why she didn't pick up my first phone calls. She said they had gotten into a fight. He made her cry, and she went to the bathroom. Upon her return, she noticed him playing with her phone, but Lilly had no idea he'd sent anything," I explain to her. I feel sick. What the hell have I done?

"Oh, Luca …" Natalia says as she reaches out and grabs my hand, understanding the reason I've turned myself into the Playboy Prince again was because I thought Lilly was done with me.

I fucked up.

"She said she tried to call me after he left. That she wanted to tell me something, but then …"

I punch the seat again.

"Luca, calm down," my sister chastises me.

"I blocked Lilly, then fucked someone else when she was at home waiting for me to call her back, hoping that I still felt the same way as her." My eyes close as I try to rein in my anger. "She still loved me, Natalia. I know that's what she was calling to tell me. Now I have fucked it up. I've fucked up so much." Damn my fucking ego right to hell.

"No, her ex fucked you both over. This isn't your fault," she tries to reassure me.

"We'd be together now if …"

Natalia squeezes my hand. "I know. You can't change the past, brother, but you can rewrite the future," she says, trying to placate me.

"She told me her life is here, and mine is there."

"From what we heard today, she's a brilliant doctor.

Everyone at the clinic was raving about her. She seems like a wonderful woman, Luca."

Everyone around the clinic did speak highly about her, and at the time, I hated hearing it. Hated that everyone else got her laughter, her smile, her compassion, her love, except me.

"She's doing good work for the charity," Natalia states.

"So, you're saying what? That I should leave her be?"

Never. I can't. She is buried deep inside my soul, and no matter how hard I try she's still there.

My sister's face softens. "I think you have had a shock today. That has changed the way you have been feeling all year."

I have hated Lilly for so long, and now? Now what? I find out my hate is all based on a lie.

"I think you need to let this whole situation sink in before you do anything else," Natalia suggests.

"It's hard when, for the first time, my heart has started beating again," I tell her.

Natalia lays her head on my shoulder. "You have waited this long. What's a little longer?"

Maybe she's right.

"First things first, I'm going to deal with Lilly's ex," I tell her.

"I bet you will." Natalia chuckles.

※ ※ ※ ※

> Luca: I've dealt with Rob.

> Lilly: Please tell me he is still alive?

> Lilly: Luca!!

Chuckling to myself as I tease her, I type out another message.

Luca: Yes, he's alive. But he might not be after I sent his girlfriend copies of all the messages he's sent to other women.

Lilly: What a dick! Will he never learn?

Luca: Doesn't look like it.

Lilly: Why are men such idiots?

Luca: Not all men.

Lilly: All men have an idiot buried inside of them. Just have to wait for the right situation and out they come.

Luca: You're probably right.

Lilly: Thanks for unblocking me to share this good news.

Yep. I'm officially an idiot, and that was my biggest idiotic moment of all time.

How do I apologize for the misunderstanding?

Luca: You know I'm sorry about that.

Lilly: I know you are. It was one giant mess.

Luca: I wanted to kill him for what he did to us.

Lilly: It's hard to not think what could have been.

Oh good, I'm not alone in thinking this way.

This is a good start.

Luca: Doesn't mean it can't be again.

Just say the word, Lilly.

The silence that came after that text message was deafening.

* * * *

A couple of days later came the perfect opportunity for me to text Lilly again as she'd just moved to Albania for her promotion. I'm proud of her. And this promotion has nothing to do with me, she earned it.

> Luca: How's Albania?

> Lilly: It's gorgeous. But fucking cold.

This makes me chuckle.

> Luca: Settling in okay.

> Lilly: Yeah. Everyone seems lovely. I'm pretty excited to get stuck into the work. I know I can't save everyone, but I must try.

I love that she is so passionate about the cause.

> Luca: Those girls have the best woman looking after them. You are going to change their lives.

> Lilly: Stop it! You're making me cry.

> Luca: I'm proud of you, Lil. I've heard nothing but praise from everyone you have worked with.

> Lilly: Have you been checking up on me?

> Is she teasing, or is she upset?

> Luca: I neither confirm nor deny.

> Lilly: Spoken like a true politician.

> Luca: The palace is separate from the state.

> Lilly: Oh, you're good. Divert. Divert. Divert. lol

Phew, she is teasing.

> Luca: Do you have plans for Christmas?

> Lilly: No, I'll be working.

> Luca: Have you seen your sister recently?

> Lilly: No, not in almost a year. Been saving lives and stuff. She understands, though.

This gives me the perfect idea to perhaps get back into Lilly's good graces.

28

LUCA

I'm getting ready to go to my parents' home for Christmas Eve when my phone rings. **'Lilly'** is displayed on the screen—it looks like she got my Christmas present.

"Merry Christmas," I answer the phone with a giant smile on my face even though she can't see.

"You ... I ... how the hell did you do this?" she asks, stumbling over her words.

"Thanks, Luca," Laura calls out in the background. She sounds happy.

"I couldn't let you have another Christmas without your sister," I tell her.

The phone line goes quiet except for what sounds like sniffles.

"Thank you ..." she hiccups through her tears, "... I don't know how I can repay you for this?"

"You owe me nothing, Lilly," I say. Just knowing how happy she is, is more than enough for me.

"Thank you, thank you, thank you ..." she repeats over and over again with a smile in her voice. "This is going to be the best Christmas ever. Except ..."

My stomach sinks. What did I miss?

"Except what?"

"Except you're not here."

The phone goes quiet for a few seconds.

Then she backtracks. "I'm sorry, Luca, I shouldn't have said that. I got carried away by your thoughtful gift."

"I wish I was. I'd give anything to be there with you," I confess.

"You would?"

"Yeah, I miss you, Lilly," I tell her. I need her to know that.

"I miss you too, Luca," she confesses.

"I can't get there to see you until after the new year," I explain. Cursing my calendar and all the engagements I said yes to, purely to keep my mind off Lilly.

"There's no rush. Maybe we should take our time," she tells me.

"I'd like that. Do you mind if I call you again?" I ask.

The first time we were together, we went from zero to one hundred damn quickly. Now that I know there's a chance between us, we have all the time in the world.

"I'd like that, a lot. Merry Christmas, Luca."

"Merry Christmas, Lilly," I say with a smile on my face. I hang up the phone.

❄ ❄ ❄ ❄

Over the holidays, we speak every day. Yeah, I know, we said we should go slow, but when it came to it, it was kind of hard to do.

"You seem happier," My mama says, taking a seat beside me on the sofa. We're about to ring in the new year.

I can't believe how much has happened in one short year. This time last year I was snuggled up with Lilly in Edinburgh.

"I am," I answer, taking a sip from the whisky tumbler in my hand.

"Is it the doctor?" My mother questions me.

I shouldn't be surprised that my mother knows what's going on with me, even when I haven't told her. She has eyes and ears everywhere.

"Don't look at me like that. It's my job to know what's happening with all my children. Plus, Natalia filled me in," she says, giving me a smile.

Natalia, that little gossip. "Lilly and I have reconnected. After a lot of miscommunications and some sabotage from her ex."

Mama nods. "She has a good reputation at the charity for her hard work."

Of course, she has checked up on her.

"She's amazing."

"Your face lights up when you speak about her," she says as she reaches over and squeezes my thigh.

"I want to get it right this time. My feelings haven't changed since the moment I met her a year ago. It was strong and intense from the start, and both of us let outside influences make us think what we felt wasn't real. I can't lose her again," I confess to her.

"I'm sorry things between you and Lilly didn't work out the way you may have planned. Least now after everything you have been through you know the feelings the two of you have for each other are true."

I could have done without this year-long test.

"You know she'll have to give up her job if you want to marry her," my mother warns me.

This is a fact, and this is what I'm afraid of. Looking over at my mother, she knows that I am worried that if Lilly had to make a choice between being a doctor and marrying me, I'm not sure I would win.

"She could still deal with the causes, but she could not be on the frontline like she is now," my mother explains.

"That's what I'm worried about," I confess to her.

"Her calling is strong, *my dear.* And I know this would be one of the reasons that could make your relationship difficult."

"I can't let her go again," I say.

She reaches out and cups my face. "Give her the choice. Do not take that away from her. Be prepared for her not to give you the answer you may want, but, above all, be patient. She has worked all her life to become a doctor. When the time is right for her, she will choose you," my mother explains.

Maybe she's right. We're both still young, we have plenty of time.

✳ ✳ ✳ ✳

"Luca, Luca," Natalia screams as she rushes into my apartment.

"Where's the fire?" I ask her.

Natalia glares at me.

"Luca …" Giorgio calls out, he isn't far behind her.

The look on their faces tells me something serious has happened.

"What is it? Is it Papá?" I ask, looking between my siblings.

They shake their heads.

"It's Lilly," Natalia states.

What?

No.

I only spoke to her this morning.

"Tell me? What's happened?" I yell at them both as panic laces every inch of my body as I wait.

"Lilly's been kidnapped," Giorgio states.

My world begins to crumble around me. The shock of his words makes me stumble for a moment.

"Kidnapped?" I repeat the word as bile rises in my throat and a light sheen of sweat forms across my forehead.

No.

No.

No.

"She was supposed to be safe. Why wasn't she safe? I told you I needed her to be safe," I scream at my brother as my anger bubbles to the surface and my fists ball tightly.

"She was safe," Natalia adds.

"All we know so far is that she sacrificed herself," Giorgio informs me.

She did what? No. Tell me she wouldn't be this stupid.

"She's alive. She has to be," I scream at them.

Giorgio and Natalia both look at each other with pain etched across their faces.

No.

Please, God, no.

I should've told her I still loved her this morning. It was on the tip of my tongue, but things have been going so well this past month. I didn't want to jinx anything. I should have told her. She needed to know I love her. I want to be with her. She needs to have something to fight for. I need her to come back to me. I can't lose her again. Falling to my knees with the weight of the world on me, my head falls into my hands. This can't be happening not when I've finally got her back.

"Luca," Natalia says softly, wrapping her arms around me. "We haven't had confirmation so there's still hope."

Turning, I look at my sister through watery eyes. "I still love her."

Natalia wraps her arms around me tighter. "I know you do."

Once the initial shock wore off, Giorgio, Natalia, and I headed to the emergency briefing at the charity's headquarters. Lilly has been working in an Albanian women's health clinic in a small town called Tropojë which borders with Kosovo Republic or Serbia, depending on which side of the conflict you're on. Lilly loves being able to make a difference in the women's lives who have been saved because of the charity.

We're ushered into the boardroom filled with people in suits, all looking tense. There are a couple of men in military uniforms and some junior staff running around doing things for their bosses. When we entered the room, everyone stood, bowed, then sat down.

The Director of the Board explains that the women's clinic was stormed by men dressed in paramilitary-looking uniforms. He then clicks onto the smartboard in front of him and brings up the security footage.

Natalia reaches under the table and holds my hand as I watch, in grainy black and white, the worst horror movie of my life. In slow motion, the men point their automatic weapons at our team. Right there at the front is Lilly with fear written all over her face.

Fuck!

I squeeze Natalia's hand tighter as we watch in silence at the events unfolding before our very eyes. I watch as one of the men grabs a female doctor and throws her to the ground, hard. Blood begins to pour from a wound on her head. They are shouting at the group when someone steps forward to help the woman on the ground, but they get a gun pointed at their head.

Lilly is the one that steps forward to help the woman, and I watch in disbelief as a gun is pointed directly at her.

Whoever that fucker is, I'm going to kill him.

Her hands are shaking. That's the only outward sign that she's scared because her face shows determination when she says something to the men. Two of them turn to discuss something, then one of them reaches out and grabs Lilly. The woman on the floor is crying and screaming as they drag Lilly away.

The director explains that witnesses advised that Lilly Simpson offered herself instead because the doctor they wanted to take had two small children at home.

Fuck, Lilly. Why the hell do you have to be a martyr?

We continue to listen, but it doesn't take me long before I'm storming out of the headquarters and to my town car.

"Bunch of incompetent fools," I say as I slam my fist against the bulletproof glass. "They're going to get her killed going through all that fucking red tape."

"Their hands are tied, Luca. The charity has protocols," Natalia reminds me.

"Fuck them! I don't. I don't have fucking protocols. I don't care how much it's going to cost … I need to get her home. I don't care how we do it or even who does it. She needs to be home. Safe." I thump my chest. "With me."

The car is silent for a couple of moments.

"I know people who can help," Giorgio says as he looks up at me. "They know how the Bratva works, especially the human trafficking side. They have rescued many women from them before this."

Hope blooms as Giorgio tells me more.

"They are based out of Ibiza. They might be your only hope."

"Then do it. I don't care how much it costs. I want her home, now!"

That night my dreams are filled with nightmares. Images of Lilly being taken from the clinic, of blood and gunshots have me waking up in a cold sweat.

Getting out of bed, I grab a bottle of water and look out over my balcony at the ancient buildings.

"Please don't hurt her," I say on a prayer.

Resting my head against the cool brick, suddenly, an idea hits me. I remember I still have her phone number in my system when I was a crazy stalker. Rushing to my laptop, I open it and click on the app.

"Please, please, have your phone on you, Lilly."

The screen turns on, but there's no longer a blinking light, which means her phone isn't turned on anymore.

Fuck.

I click a couple more links, and it shows me exactly where she was last—Kosovo.

At least now we have a place to start.

We'll find you, Lilly.

That, I promise.

29

LILLY

I *don't want to die.*

The words are on a loop inside my brain.

My hands are tied behind my back as soon as we're outside the clinic. A bag is put over my head, and I'm shoved into a waiting truck. My heart feels like it's going to launch right out of my chest, the thundering beat echoing through my brain.

The rumble of the engine starts and vibrates through me. When we take off, I slide across the chair and hit my shoulder against the cold hard steel.

I don't want to die.

We travel along bumpy roads. The suspension on the truck is bad as I bounce all over the place.

Where the hell are we going?

I've been trying to calm myself down. Knowing that having a clear mind will help me survive being kidnapped. When you're panicking, you don't remember things, things that could ultimately save your life. But it is so fucking hard. I'm so scared.

I slow my breathing down and try to remember every little thing about what just happened. It seemed to happen so fast, it felt more like a blur. I concentrate and try to remember every tiny detail.

I've only been in Albania for a short time, but I have picked up a little bit of their language. Enough anyway to deal with the basics in women's health, but I don't think it's the same words as the kidnappers. Concentrating hard, I try and see if I can pinpoint anything about what these men are saying.

Why the hell do I not know anything about guns? That may help me. The guns they were holding appeared big and black. Yeah, that could be any type of gun, I have no idea.

What are they wearing?

All black military—top, pants, I think Kevlar chest plates, ski masks—your typical standard bad-guy gear.

Now isn't the time for jokes, Lilly.

But if I don't laugh, I'll cry.

No, don't do either. You'll have a full-on mental breakdown and probably get yourself killed for being hysterical.

Think, Lilly, think.

One of them had a tattoo on his forehand. I noticed it when he had the gun pointing at Mariana.

Think, Lilly.

My mind is fuzzy and the image is blurry.

A star. He had a star.

I remember when I first started, the team told me what the different tattoos meant, especially on the women. They told me that if I saw a man with a ten-pointed star that they were Bratva or Russian mafia and to be very careful.

Oh shit, that's what I saw.

I'm in a truckload of trouble.

Panic begins to take over.

My chest tightens and the binds around my wrists begin to cut into me.

Keep it together, Lilly.

Keep it together.

✳ ✳ ✳ ✳

After what seems like forever, the truck finally stops. The crunch of boots on gravel echo around me, then the screech of the truck doors opening gains my attention. Someone yells at me in a language I don't understand. When their hands land on me, I jump. I still have the bag over my head and can't see a thing. Whoever they are pulls me up and drags me across the truck, then throw me off the edge.

Fucking hell, I'm going to die.

Someone catches me before I can hit the ground. The men chuckle at my screams.

I'm righted once again and dragged along the gravel, which I'm assuming is a pathway. The gravel turns into concrete or stone, I'm not sure which. The sound of stomping boots is all around me. There's no way I can escape. I don't even know where I am.

The temperature changes from the frigid cold of the harsh winter to tropical heat. We must be inside now. I'm pushed hard in the back, my feet tripping over each other, and I land on my knees hard, scraping them through my jeans. Momentum has me falling forward, my forehead hitting the carpet.

It's going to be okay, Lilly.

Trying to calm myself down. *You'll be okay if you are calm. They need you for something. Then they are going to let you go again. You need to survive. Do as you're told, then you can go home and put this whole mess behind you.*

There's shouting suddenly, then the sound of flesh hitting flesh echoes around me. Squeezing my eyes shut, I attempt to block the dreadful sounds. The next moment, the rope around my wrists has been cut, and my hood is removed.

It takes my eyes a while to adjust as I slowly sit up on my heels. Blinking a couple of times, a man's face comes into focus. He's smiling while holding out a hand to me. He has slick black hair, bright blue eyes, and a scar that runs down the right side of his cheek with a square jaw and the start of some stubble. He's dangerously handsome which is very off-putting. Bad guys aren't supposed to look like *GQ* models. He's dressed in a black dress suit, the sleeves rolled up his thick, tanned arms covered in intricate tattoos.

"I'm so sorry that my men have treated you so poorly. Believe me, they'll be dealt with accordingly. They disobeyed my instructions," he says with a thick Russian accent.

My eyes widen because I can hear the undercurrent of a threat in his words.

"Please ..." he says, holding out his hand to me.

I take it, and it's surprisingly warm as he helps me onto my unsteady legs. They falter for a moment, but his strong hands are wrapped around my hips, a little too closely for my liking. Now that I'm standing, I realize how tall and broad he is. He could break me in two in seconds if he wanted. I don't think I should be reassured by his good looks. He is, without a doubt, a very bad man.

He takes a couple of steps away from me and grabs something. "Here, drink this," he says as he hands me a bottled water.

Reluctantly I take it. Is he going to drug me? I stare at the plastic bottle, not game enough to take a sip. I've heard from women that the water bottles are usually spiked.

"Drink. You must be thirsty," his deep voice commands.

I stare at the bottle debating if I should or not.

His blue eyes narrow at me, then he realizes what I'm thinking. "Miss, I assure you no harm is going to come to you under my watch."

Yeah, whatever, I'm not convinced. I've seen his face now, so what's to stop him from killing me? Isn't that what usually happens in the movies?

He takes the bottle of water from my hand, opens it, and takes a sip before handing it back to me. "See, okay?"

Reluctantly, I take a small sip.

He reaches out suddenly and grabs my wrists checking the rope burn. His thumb runs over the bloodied marks. "I'm sorry. This should not have happened." He continues to touch me, making me feel uncomfortable.

I pull my hands away from him. "Why am I here?" The question sounds timid on my lips.

"We need your help." Those blue eyes of his stare at me intensely.

"Why did you kidnap me if you needed help?" I ask him.

"Because it was the only way to buy your silence," he confesses, crossing his large arms across his chest as he raises a dark brow at me.

"I took an oath as a doctor that no matter what, I'll help anyone," I tell him.

He stares at me. "Can't take risks in my job."

"If I help, are you going to let me go?" That was a stupid question, Lilly. Of course, he is going to say yes. Otherwise, you won't help him if you know you're going to die.

"Yes. I promise you. My word is law around here," he says seriously.

For some reason, I believe him. Taking another sip of the water, I steady myself. "I don't care about anything else except helping people in need."

I'll make sure to take in every bit of detail and information there is about this place just in case I need it.

Those blue eyes narrow on me, assessing me, making sure I'm telling the truth. What he must see is enough for him to trust me. "Very good. Follow me," he says as he turns on his heel and walks out of the room.

I follow behind him hurriedly because of his long strides. We head down a long corridor, and he opens the last door on the left and indicates for me to enter.

Everything stops.

There is row upon row of girls in a makeshift dorm room. There must be easily thirty women, all various ages, all slender, all Eastern European-looking. When the door opens, the women freeze, but worse when they see the man with me, some of them try and hide from his view. They are one hundred percent scared of him. He pushes me into the room and shuts the door behind him.

"They need check-ups," he states, his voice is hard and to the point.

The girls' eyes are wide, but no one dares move. "Sexual health check-ups?" I question.

"Yes. I want to make sure none of them have diseases," he says.

He wants to make sure his purchases are clean before selling them. My stomach rolls around in disgust. This is everything I have been fighting against. This asshole is someone I'm trying to eradicate from this world.

He must see something in me change because he leans down close to my ear and whispers, "I promised you no harm will come to you if you do as you're told. Stray from that, and there's a spare bed waiting for you."

Ice runs through my veins upon hearing his words, and I know he will. He has nothing to lose. No one knows where I am, and if they do, he can easily move me to anywhere in the world with a single click of his fingers.

"Is that all you need from me?" I ask.

The asshole shakes his head. "Follow me." He opens the door again and takes me down another long corridor. This time he opens a metal door, and I'm greeted with a makeshift maternity ward.

Holy fucking shit!

There must be twenty babies in here with very frail, young women beside them. Some of them are playing with their babies, others are lying lifeless, staring at the ceiling.

These poor women.

"I need you to check the babies and the women over. I need to know how long till they can work again."

What? No. I won't do that. Is this some kind of baby factory? My stomach turns. I've seen the aftermath of women forced back into this kind of work after giving birth. The long-term effects on their bodies and their mental health problems.

"The minimum time is six weeks for a vaginal birth, longer if it's cesarean," I explain to him. Dear God, I hope none of the girls have had to have a cesarean. This room does not look like it's equipped for that type of surgery.

"Six weeks?" his voice raises.

Turning to him, I reiterate, "Yes. Six weeks. Maybe if you made the men wear protection or the women go on birth control, then you wouldn't have this problem."

His blue eyes widen and his nostrils flare.

I sink a little inside myself at his stare.

Fuck him.

I'm doing him a favor, and he can damn well listen to me. I straighten my back, he's not going to intimidate me. If I can't save these girls, I sure as hell am going to make sure I can at least stop any long-term damage happening to them. "If you treated the women better, then you would have fewer problems."

"Women are easy to find," he says as he raises a defiant brow in my direction.

"Yes, but then you have to train them all over again. How many women do you lose because they're new?" I question him.

Play this right, Lilly.

"Depends. But I'd say around thirty percent of the new women are lost," he replies so casually.

I've never wanted to murder someone before until now, but this asshole standing in front of me, I could easily slit his throat. Fuck the Hippocratic Oath and all its righteous bullshit!

"How much does it cost to acquire a girl?"

Easy does it now, Lilly.

"About one thousand American dollars," he states.

Is human life worth so little?

"Did you know implanting a contraceptive only costs around one hundred dollars."

Those blue eyes narrow at me, but he doesn't say anything.

"Seems like a saving, doesn't it? Especially if women are out for six weeks giving birth, if not more."

"I'm not sure what you're playing at, doc," he says. His words turn like ice, and his face goes blank.

"I can't stop what you're doing here …" I tell him as I wave my hand through the air, "… but I can, at least, help these women live a better life."

"You care that much about these whores?" he questions me.

Stay calm, Lilly. Stay calm.

"I'm sure most of them didn't have dreams about becoming whores," I say, biting back.

The asshole bursts out laughing. "It must be nice to live in that gilded cage you occupy, doc. Looking down from your high-in-the-sky perch while thinking that people like me are the scum of the earth," he says with a sneer.

Stay strong, Lilly. Don't say anything.

"What these women are doing is helping their families. The money they earn goes back to them, helping them keep a roof over their heads, food on the table, and siblings in school. They have sacrificed their lives for their families," the man states.

Hold the tears in, Lilly.

"Can't you make the sacrifice worth it, then?" My comment surprises him. His tattooed finger taps his chin as he thinks over my words.

"Why should I care?" His voice is now deep and demanding information.

"Why should a farmer care about his flock when they are just going to be slaughtered?"

A small smile falls across his face. "You ..." he points his finger at me, "... you have balls, doc." He chuckles. "You're right. The better the condition of my flock, the better price I can get."

I may not be able to save them yet, but as long as the girls are healthy, that's the best I can hope for.

"I'll get you what you need, doc. Anything to make these girls better. You have my word."

And guess that is all I can hope for.

30

LUCA

"**Y**ou better let me in, so help me," a woman screeches at the front of my apartment building.

I have been for a run and still as I watch the commotion unfold.

"Signora, you aren't allowed in here. If you do not step away, I'll call the police," my security states.

"Then, I will go to the media and tell the world that your beloved prince killed my sister." The woman hisses.

Security stills at the woman's words.

Shit. That is Lilly's sister.

"Laura, come on, babe … we'll find Lilly another way. You can't end up in jail." A blond man tries to pull her away from my security.

I rush toward the entrance and call out, "Laura?"

"Where is she?" Laura screams. Her blue eyes are red-rimmed, her hair a bright rainbow of color. "Please, Luca … where is she?" she pleads with me.

Her fiancé holds her tightly as she begins to crumble.

"Let them in," I tell my security.

My security gives me a strange look but ultimately does as he's told.

"Please ... let's discuss this upstairs," I tell them.

Laura calms a little, and they follow me to my apartment. We stand in the elevator in awkward silence till we make it to my level. We all step into my apartment, and I head straight to the kitchen. I need to grab a drink after my run.

"Can I get you anything? Water, juice, coffee?" I ask.

Laura ignores my question.

"Tequila?" The blond man asks, giving me a small smile.

"Where's Lilly? Is it true what they're saying on the news that a doctor has been kidnapped? I haven't heard from her, Luca," she screams at me as tears stream down her face, and her fiancé holds her tightly.

"Yes, it's true. It's Lilly who has been taken," I tell her honestly.

"Oh, God ... no. No. She's my family, Luca. My family." She cries as she crumples to the floor.

"I know. I promise you ... I'm doing everything in my power to get her back," I tell her.

"It's been twenty-four hours. Shouldn't there be some kind of ransom or something?" Laura asks.

"We believe it's not a traditional kidnapping. They're not after money," I explain.

"Then what the hell do they want from her?" Laura's bright blue eyes remind me of Lilly so much.

You can see the family resemblance between the sisters.

"Oh God, they are going to sell her. Lilly is beautiful. Smart. She's going to be someone's ..." she trails off hysterically.

Reaching out to Laura, I grab her hands. "Nothing is going to happen to her, I promise you. They wouldn't dare touch a hair on her head."

Laura looks up at me. "You'll make them pay if they do."

"I promise you I'll burn everything to the ground if they touch her."

✳ ✳ ✳ ✳

After setting Laura and her fiancé Andy up in a hotel, I reassure them I'll keep them in the loop with anything to do with Lilly. Laura deserves to know what is going on and I feel awful not contacting her sooner. I promised her I will stop at nothing to get her sister back and she was able to calm down after that.

"Would you relax?" My brother halts my leg from bouncing with his hand.

I nervously wait for the people Giorgio recommended could help.

"They are the best. They know what they're doing, I promise," he tells me.

"How do you know them?" I ask him.

"I'm friends with Tomas Ramirez," he states.

"The property guy, who is with that Spanish actor?" I ask him.

"Mateo Vilaro, yes. Their fiancée Zoe was kidnapped by these people too as was her sister. Because of that, they have set up their own organization that rescues women from being trafficked. The charity has reached out to them a couple of times to help in situations," Giorgio explains to me.

"How did I not know about this? I'm its patron," I question my brother.

"You're the face of it, yes," he answers, and that seems condescending.

"Hey, I do more than that," I bite back.

"You have this past year, yes, especially once Lilly started working for it. You showed interest," my brother states.

Fine. He got me there. Yes, I wasn't as involved with the

charity as I am now. My priorities since breaking up with Rachele have changed, and I think for the better.

"Guys, they're here," Natalia announces as the elevator doors open.

We all stand and watch as four serious-looking people enter my apartment. A blond version of the Hulk. Another man who looks like he could simultaneously hack into your system while fighting a bear. Then there's this tiny blonde woman who gives off some sort of super scary vibe. And another blonde who looks to be the only one smiling.

"Your Highnesses ..." one of the women greets us. "It's a pleasure to meet you all. I certainly wish it was under better circumstances," she says.

Is that an Australian accent?

Who are these people?

"I'm Sophie, this is Brooks ..." she points to the hulking man, "... and this is Damon." She points to the hacker-looking guy, "And that is my sister, Mackenzie, who is here because she knows Lilly," she explains as the other blonde gives us all a sad smile.

This has my attention.

"Please, take a seat," Giorgio says as he points to the living room opposite us.

Natalia busies herself in the kitchen getting refreshments for us all.

"So how do you know Lilly?" I ask Mackenzie.

"I'm a doctor too. I did three months in Kenya working with her. We've kept in touch ever since. It hasn't been as frequent as we both would have wished for," she explains.

Wish we could have met under better circumstances. I can see the agony on her face that she wishes she had kept in touch more frequently than they must have. She will get a chance to catch up with her again soon, I know it.

"Now that's out of the way. We have looked through all the media transcripts of what's happened," Sophie starts seriously.

"We also looked into the security footage from the clinic and the surrounding areas," Damon adds, opening his laptop.

"Thank you for the information about Kosovo, that was extremely helpful," Brooks states.

"So, we have been concentrating on that area. Due to the ongoing conflict in that region, the Bratva is able to easily move without much worry," Sophie advises.

"We have a rough idea of the area and where the Bratva has safe houses, but the important places aren't so easy to find," Damon adds, showing us a map of Kosovo. "This is the last known ping from Lilly's phone."

A little green dot is highlighted on the map.

"This road here …" he points, "… is the main highway between Albania and Kosovo."

"So, she could be anywhere?" I say. I thought these people were experts.

"No. I know it doesn't look like much, and it may seem like we're searching for a needle in a haystack, but trust us, we *will* find her," Sophie attempts to reassure me.

"The good thing about all this is that Lilly is a doctor. Which means they need her for something," Brooks adds.

"She specializes in women's health, doesn't she?" Sophie asks.

I nod my head.

"They must be having problems with their girls," Mackenzie states.

My eyes widen at her words, and one in particular—girls.

"Lilly is passionate about human trafficking. That's why she was there," I explain to the team.

Sophie nods in understanding. "I'm sure you may have heard already, but both of my sisters were kidnapped by the Bratva. Unfortunately, they were on the sold side of the business. We got them back, thank goodness. But that's why we have this business because it's our passion to save women from this life."

Natalia sets down glasses of water on the table. "Do you think Lilly has a chance?" she asks.

The four of them look at each other and silently have a conversation before answering.

"Yes. If she's smart and does what she is told," Sophie advises me. "If she tries to escape, they'll kill her."

Fuck!

Running my hand through my hair, I think, *Please, Lilly, don't be brave. I'm coming for you.*

"Most people who have been kidnapped think they'll try and escape, but in reality, they never do," Brooks advises.

"Like I said, Lilly is a doctor, and that's a hot commodity to have. She could be there to save the boss's life, his wife, his child, or maybe he's doing the right thing and looking after the girls he has. We don't know yet, and that's the million-dollar question," Sophie states as she tries to sound positive.

"How long do you think it will take to get her back?" I ask.

The four of them look at each other, and I don't like the looks they are sharing.

"It's hard to say. There are many variables in this scenario. I don't want to give you false hope," Sophie explains.

Shit.

"We're the best," Sophie reminds me.

"Good, because I need you to get back the woman I love," I tell them.

※ ※ ※ ※

"They are going to bring Lilly home, Luca," Natalia says as she curls into me on the sofa.

"They are the best, Luca," Giorgio reassures me.

"I should never have let her go," I say as I press a kiss to my sister's head.

"You didn't know something like this would happen," Giorgio adds.

"Yeah, but I still loved her. And I should have done more," I tell them both.

"Luca ..." Natalia looks up at me, tears welling in her eyes, "... she's coming home. You two will be together again, I can feel it."

I wish I had the same damn faith as Natalia.

Letting my head fall back against the sofa, my mind wanders to Lilly.

Is she safe?

31

LILLY

I have been here for one week.

Seven days.

One hundred and sixty-eight hours.

Living in a damn nightmare.

Every day, I implant girl after girl with birth control. Each one of them looks gaunt, lifeless, and broken. I don't know how many women are at this facility. I have lost count.

My nights are spent crying myself to sleep. I don't sleep much only in small amounts, even though they have set me up in a plush apartment where all I can see out the windows are row upon row of what looks to be warehouses, hidden behind thick forest.

There are two armed guards by my door inside and outside. The windows in my apartment are bolted shut.

Where the hell would I even go if I were able to escape?

I'd die of hyperthermia before I had a chance to go anywhere. We're in the middle of winter. One night spent out there in below-zero temperatures, and I'd be dead.

Every single day is the same. I wake up and breakfast is slid through a flap in the door which consists of a slice of bread, pastries, coffee, and juice. They give me twenty minutes to eat my breakfast and be ready for the day. An armed guard then escorts me from my apartment across the graveled parking area and into one of the large warehouses.

They have reorganized the makeshift hospital for me. The latest equipment was brought in—state-of-the-art everything. Then, one by one the girls come in. Many fear me and hardly any speak English.

There's one girl, Ilona, so I asked if she could be my interpreter. Eventually, I got my way, and she was able to stay with me. It's nice having someone to talk to in this damn hellhole. She's explained her circumstances to me—twenty, studying at a university in Moscow to be a doctor. Unfortunately, her brother is a drug addict and owed the Bratva a lot of money. They killed him and are making her work off his debt. She has been here for one year.

"Thank you for helping us," Ilona says, giving me a small smile. "The girls have been talking at night, and they think you're their guardian angel."

Shaking my head, tears well in my eyes. "Don't say that. I can't save you. Not yet, anyway. I'm no angel."

Ilona reaches out and holds my hand. "You're helping us. Our biggest worry is having a baby here. When you have one, they take it away from you."

I found this out on day two working in the maternity ward, and it made me physically ill.

"We know the baby isn't made out of love, but … it's still our flesh and blood," She says.

"I'm sorry I can't do more," I tell her.

"Miss Lilly … you are. You have given us all hope."

How can these girls have hope in a place like this?

"We feel protected now. We can make it through this night-mare," she explains to me.

Tears fall down my cheeks as I pull Ilona in for a hug. "I

promise you … as soon as I get out, I'm going to come back for you. Do you hear me?"

"Do not worry about us, Miss Lilly. We'll be fine," she says quietly.

The door swings open, and an armed guard screams something, I have no idea what.

"Our time is up. Till tomorrow, Miss Lilly," Ilona says.

I watch as the guard violently hauls Ilona away, the door slamming behind them.

I sterilize my utensils before putting them all away.

"You've been doing a good job. The girls seem much happier." The good-looking bad guy walks in. He has never given me his name, and I understand why because that would mean I'd know too much. But one day I'll find out, and make sure he pays for this nightmare place.

"I told you I would do my job."

"Yes, it seems you have kept your part of the bargain," he says.

I don't think he's used to saying that to many people. I can tell by the look in his eyes.

"Those women are human beings. I know you don't see them that way, but they, too, deserve some sort of dignity in this shitty life they have been dealt," I tell him.

That was the wrong thing to say because quick as a flash, his hand wraps around my throat, his fingers slowly closing around it. Panic runs through my veins as I find it harder to breathe.

"Know your place, woman." Those blue eyes swirl with violence and hatred. "Do not overstep your mark."

Slowly, I nod, letting him know I understand. But he doesn't let go of me, his fingers ease ever so slightly.

"I bet you're feisty in bed," he says, licking his lips.

No. No. No. My eyes widen in sheer terror.

"Don't panic, I'll not touch you … unless you want me to." He smirks while I shake my head slowly. "Maybe not yet but soon." Those eyes sparkle with desire as he continues, "I'm not ready to let you go, yet. I like having you around."

Wait. What? No.

"You intrigue me too much." His hand falls from my throat, and I fall back trying to catch my breath.

"I'm no one special." The words come out as barely a whisper.

He takes a step forward, and I flinch at his movement, which he ignores. His finger comes under my chin making me look up at him. "I think you're extraordinary."

Then, after dropping that bombshell, he stalks away from the hospital, the metal door slamming shut behind him, the sound echoing through the empty room.

I need to get out of here and back to my room.

After a steaming hot shower to try and rid myself of his evil touch, I look in the mirror, and there are the faintest of bruises around my neck where he tried to strangle me. I stare out into the darkness that has now fallen across the outside world and wonder how my sister is, how Luca is, but those thoughts just bring me more pain so I quickly shut them away.

Dinner's some weird soup, but I'm starving, so I don't care and finish it quickly.

Now, I lie on the bed and stare at the ceiling, willing myself to wake up from this never-ending nightmare.

Has the world forgotten about me?

Why has no one come for me?

My thoughts flick back to Laura—she must be beside herself with worry. She better not do something stupid and try to rescue me. The problem is, I wouldn't put it past her. Even though I know how dangerous this thought is, it still makes me smile.

I wonder if Luca's concerned. We had been getting closer since that day in Brindisi. Little by little, we were overcoming the shitstorm Rob created between us.

A fresh start.

I miss him so much.

A single tear falls down my cheek remembering his beautiful face.

If I ever get out of here, I'll never let him go again.

32

LILLY

A cold, leather hand wraps around my mouth in the darkness, pulling me from my sleep. I'm unable to scream as I'm lifted off the bed.

What the hell is going on?

Whoever has me, I attempt to kick and land a good one on his shin.

"Stop it," the man grunts. "I'm trying to fucking save you."

I still at his coarse tone.

Save me?

"She's going to freeze out there," another male voice speaks.

I can't tell how many people are in my room because of how dark it is, but I notice the red lights at the tips of their guns.

Guns!

"Shit," the man holding me curses. "Lilly Simpson ...." *He knows my name.* "If I let go of your mouth, do you promise not to scream?" I nod. "We're friends of Luca Fiorenzo."

My eyes widen with surprise.

Luca.

They've been sent by Luca.

Nodding furiously, the man lets go of me. I hurry over to my

bare closet, grab my socks and shoes, and quickly put them on.
Then I grab a sweater and pop it over my head.

Luca.

Luca has come to save me.

"Come, we have to go, now. We have a window of maybe ten
minutes before shit is about to go down."

You don't have to tell me twice. I follow their lead out the
front door of my apartment.

Weird. There is no …

That's when I see it, my two guards are laid out on the floor.

We carefully creep along the corridor, then down the stairs.
The front door opens easily, and I see another two guards on the
floor.

"We came through the forest. It's going to be rough going
for a bit, but I promise you, you're safe," the deep voice
tells me.

"Okay," I squeak out.

The guys make a couple of hand gestures, and then we're off
through the forest. I can't see a thing, but I follow eagerly behind
the person in front of me. It feels like forever to get to the road
where I can see a van waiting for us. The door swings open, and
we all jump in.

"Go, go, go …" one of them screams.

The van takes off while someone shuts the door mid-escape.

"You're safe now, Lilly." The passenger turns, taking off her
ski mask. A beautiful blonde woman smiles warmly at me. "I'm
Sophie, and we're taking you home," she says.

A sob falls from my lips as the stress of the past week
catches up with me.

The man dressed in dark military gear beside me places his
arm around my shoulders as I break down.

I must fall asleep at some point because I wake up at the jolt
of the van stopping.

How long have I been out?

The sun is rising as I slowly sit up and look out the tinted windows, and the first thing I see is an airplane.

"We're here." Sophie turns around and grins. "You better go because there's someone very eager to see you."

The sliding door of the van opens, the smell of jet fuel fills my nostrils, and then I see him, dressed in dark jeans and a white woolen sweater standing at the top of the stairs of a private plane.

"Lilly," he screams.

Hearing my name on his lips again is too much, and tears begin to fall as he rushes down the stairs toward me.

I should never have given him up.

"Lilly." He pulls me into his arms, and it feels right. This feels like home.

Why was I so stupid?

Wrapping his strong arms around me, he holds me tightly, and never in my life have I ever felt this safe.

Luca sucks in a deep breath in my hair. "I never thought I was going to see you again."

I must be honest, neither did I.

Moving my head from his chest, I look up into his tear-soaked chocolate eyes.

I'm home.

"Time to roll out, guys." Sophie makes a hand gesture.

Luca grabs my hand tightly as if he never wants to let it go again and heads up the stairs, and we step into the plush cabin. He pulls me to the back where there are two oversized seats hidden from the view of the rest of the cabin. He sits and pulls me into his side.

"I've been going crazy." His entire body is tense. "Fuck, I thought I'd lost you." Luca looks down at me, tears flowing freely down his cheeks. "I prayed every night that I'd see you again."

This man. Why was I so stupid to push him away?

His eyes widen then narrow. He reaches out and touches my neck. Oh shit, the bruises.

"Who do this to you?" he asks. That look he's giving me is pure devastation.

"I'm okay. No one touched me like that," I reassure him.

His face relaxes. "This looks like someone had their hand around your neck."

"I'm okay, Luca. Really," I try to reassure him.

"I'm sorry, Lilly."

"You have nothing to be sorry about," I tell him as I curl into his side.

Luca cups my cheek, his thumb moving my tears away. "I do. I pushed you away. My ego got the better of me."

"That doesn't matter anymore. I'm home now, and I am safe," I say, reassuring him.

"I never want to let you go again," he tells me.

"I don't want you to ever let me go, either," I tell him honestly. I snuggle into his side, and it feels so right being back in his arms, feeling his warmth and his hard plains against me.

He leans over and kisses my forehead.

This is where I'm supposed to be.

"I never stopped loving you," he whispers against my temple.

"I never stopped loving you, either, Luca."

33

LUCA

L illy fell asleep in my arms all the way home to Rome. She didn't stir even when we landed, or when I picked her up and put her into the car, or when we arrived home and I laid her in her bed.

"Where is she?" Laura screams as she rushes through the door of my apartment in a panic.

"She's sleeping," I say in a lowered tone. "I don't think she was able to sleep much."

Laura nods in agreement. "Is she okay?"

I know exactly what she's asking. Did they hurt her?

"Physically, she seems okay. It might be too early to know yet if there are any lasting problems," I explain to her.

"Thank you." Laura hugs me. "Thank you for bringing my sister back," she says through her tears.

"I still love her, Laura," I confess to her.

"I know." She gives me a watery smile.

"Should never have let her go. I promise I'm going to make it up to her." I need her to know that.

"I know she still loves you. Always has. She was scared," Laura explains to me.

"I want forever with her. I never want to know what it's like to lose her ever again," I tell her.

A large smile falls across her face. "I'm really happy for you. Welcome to the family," she says as she hugs me tightly again, and it makes me laugh for the first time in ages. I haven't been able to laugh since Lilly went missing. I feel the muscles in my body beginning to uncurl now she is safe and well in my home.

"Do you mind if I just go and check on her? I need to see her. Make sure it's real, and she's in there. I won't wake her," Laura asks.

I point her toward the bedroom. I know she must need reassurance that the nightmare is over.

Moments later, Giorgio and Natalia arrive at my apartment.

"She's home?" Natalia rushes into my arms.

"She is," I say.

"Good work," Giorgio says as he slaps me on the shoulder. "Mama and Papà send their regards," he adds.

"Is she okay?" There's concern in Natalia's question.

"On the outside, I think so."

"We can send over Dr. Regio if you want?" my brother asks.

"Maybe later. I don't want to overwhelm her just yet," I tell him.

"I can't wait to meet her." Natalia excitedly claps her hands together, and her smile is so wide her eyes are sparkling with intensity.

"Maybe another day, Natalia. I think we should leave them to it." Giorgio wraps his arm around our sister's shoulders and begins to escort her out.

She blows me a couple of kisses as the elevator doors close.

Walking back toward my bedroom to check in on Lilly, I can hear Lilly crying while her sister tries to soothe her.

"It was horrible, Laura. I couldn't save them. Any of them," she says with sniffles.

"Sweetie, I know. Sometimes the world sucks, and bad

people prosper, but what you did for them will make the shitty cards they have been dealt a little better," Laura explains to her.

What did she do?

"I should've been able to do more, Laura. It's not fair. Look at this room, it's so opulent." My stomach sinks upon hearing her words. "I can't live here like this when they have nothing."

Oh no.

"Just because you have nice things doesn't mean you don't care," Laura tries to reassure my girl.

"You don't get it," Lilly bites, sounding angry at her sister. "No one will get it because they didn't have to live through it."

Maybe I should give Dr. Regio a call?

"I'm tired, I think I might go back to sleep," she tells Laura.

Silence fills the room. Then I watch as a broken-hearted Laura steps out, shutting the door behind her. She looks up at me and breaks down. Rushing to me, she cries into my shoulder.

"I'm going to get her help. I think she's more traumatized by this than we expected. Give her time," I try to reassure her.

Laura nods, then heads out of the apartment.

※ ※ ※ ※

I must have fallen asleep on the sofa because I'm woken up by terrified screaming. Rushing toward my bedroom, I almost rip the door off its hinges to get in there where I find Lilly thrashing around the bed.

"Lilly. Lilly, it's me … Luca. You're safe." I try to soothe her.

She lashes out and scratches me across the face.

Jumping back, I stand there making sure she is all right.

She sits up in bed and takes a couple of moments to realize where she is and what just happened. "Luca?"

"I'm here," I say, stepping forward slowly so as not to startle her. I sit on the edge of the bed.

"Oh no, your face." She gasps, realizing what she's done.

Shaking my head, I reply, "It's nothing."

"I hurt you." Her face falls as she takes in the mark across my cheek.

"You were having a nightmare," I explain.

"I'm sorry." She begins to cry. "I am so sorry, Luca."

"Shhh ..." I say, comforting her as I pull her to me. "You don't have to apologize. You've been through a traumatic experience."

"He was trying to sell me," she says as she looks distraught while shaking her head from side to side. "He threatened me often that there was a bed waiting for me."

Whoever this fucker is, I'm going to make him pay for threatening her.

"He ..." She looks away.

"He what?" Her face pales as her bottom lip quivers.

"Just before I left, he told me he wasn't ready to let me go. I knew that meant he wasn't going to let me go. He also said that I intrigued him too much. That ..." she bites her bottom lip, "... that he'd be patient and wait till I gave him permission."

Every damn muscle in my body tenses.

"I didn't want him, I promise, Luca." She shakes her head.

"Shhh." I try to settle her down. "You're safe now." Holding her in my arms, I rock her back to sleep.

"Will you still love me if I'm broken?" her question is a whisper I almost don't hear.

Looking down into her bright blue eyes. "I love every bit of you, Lilly. If that means I have to slowly put you back together again, I will. Even if it takes forever."

She snuggles into me, slowly falling asleep.

34

LILLY

Mentally, it's been a lot harder than I thought it would be. I thought I was strong, but my session with Dr. Regio has helped with the post-traumatic stress syndrome I've been suffering, especially at night. Luca has been amazing, helping me struggle through it all. He has caught the brunt of some of my nightmares. Each time I wake up and see the bruises on him, it breaks my heart. He tells me not to worry, that he'll be with me as long as I need him to be and as long as I feel safe.

He's a good man.

I love him so much.

He's asked me to stay with him in Rome until I feel better. It's been a month since my return, and with the intense therapy sessions, each day is getting better.

After I got back, I asked Luca to find the warehouses and save the girls. I mean, he's a prince, he semi-owns a country, he should be able to go in and get them. He advised me it wasn't quite that easy and that it might start a war.

I get it.

But he did tell me that the people who saved me is a family-owned company that does this full-time after two of the sisters were kidnapped. That one of the sisters was an old friend Mackenzie Clark. When he told me that I couldn't believe it. Now I remember exactly what happened as she was talking to me when it went down, but she got busy with helping run the family charity that we weren't as connected as we once were. I think we need to change that. Luca tells me their organization is looking into saving the girls, but we need to give them time.

I trust them.

Finally, we got some good news. The people who saved me needed to wait a couple of weeks after rescuing me to go back in and liberate the girls. They had to make sure the way they went about it meant there were minimal casualties. I heard that they were able to rescue most of the girls and get them to a safe house, which is in Ibiza where their organization is located. Mackenzie explains that the team will monitor the girls which is her job. Helping them acclimatize back into the real world.

When they were finally able to go back to the site to try and retrieve more, unfortunately, they were not able to rescue all the girls who were there when I was. The main group had already been moved by the time they were able to get in.

Ilona was in that group.

That devastated me to hear the news. However, Mackenzie reassured me that she'd find Ilona for me. I knew if anyone could do that, they could. I asked Luca if they did find Ilona that she could come back to Italy with us. He said it would be up to Mackenzie's team to see if it was possible, but if they agreed then he didn't see why not.

I explained to him how she helped me by interpreting for me, and that she had dreams of becoming a doctor before her brother got her into the mess with the Bratva. Luca has reassured me he'll do everything in his power to have Ilona and her family move to Italy, and for her to begin her study again.

How could I not love this man?

"Morning," Luca greets me with a smile as I walk out of our bedroom. Stepping over to where he's sitting eating breakfast, I give him a big kiss. "Someone has woken up happy this morning," he says.

Sitting on his lap, I wrap my arms around his neck. "First night without nightmares."

A grin forms across his face. "I noticed." He holds me tighter.

"I feel good. Feeling more like myself."

"That's brilliant." He pulls me tighter against him.

"Thank you ... thank you for being my rock," I tell him.

"I'd do anything for you, Lilly."

Letting out a contented sigh, I know he would.

"I love you with all my heart, Luca. You've put it back together again."

He places a kiss on my temple. "You brought my heart back to life, too."

"Oh my god." Natalia comes screaming into our apartment.

"What the hell, Nat. I've told you ... you have to call before coming over," Luca chastises her.

She's walked in on us in a compromising position multiple times.

"It's worth the risk." She grins.

I can see her whole body vibrating with excitement. Natalia and I got on instantly. She felt like she already knew me from everything Luca told her about me over the year we were apart. I was a little worried at first that she might hate me for putting Luca through that, but I need not have worried, she's been amazing and so has Giorgio, his older brother. They have all been so welcoming.

I even got to meet his parents. I was so concerned because it wasn't long after I got home from the kidnapping when they came over with some of the most beautiful flowers I have ever seen. They were warm and friendly, totally different than my parents, who I haven't heard from even after they found out I had been kidnapped. That was the moment I knew they would no longer be in my life because they don't care if I'm alive or dead. It's no real loss because Luca's mother stepped in when she heard what they had done and told me now I am with Luca that I'm family. I may have cried on her shoulder, totally embarrassing myself, but she seemed fine about it.

"What's so urgent you have to interrupt our breakfast?" Luca asks angrily.

"Rachele is knocked up by Allegra's boyfriend."

Our mouths hit the floor.

"Wow, that's really messed up," I say.

Allegra has been a bitch to me since day one, but I'd never wish that kind of heartbreak on another woman.

"It is. Rachele is totally toxic, but she wouldn't believe me when I told her," Natalia says as she rolls her eyes.

"Is she okay?" Luca asks with his big-brother mode switched on.

"She's with Mama at the moment," Natalia informs us.

"Where is Tobias now?" Luca asks.

Natalia shrugs.

"Maybe Giorgio and I should pay him a little visit?" Luca says angrily.

Allegra may have done something shitty to him, but he is still going to protect her because she's his baby sister.

"Giorgio is waiting for you to call," Natalia adds with a smile.

"Right. Um …" Luca says as he looks at me.

"Go … be a big brother," I say, giving him a kiss.

He jumps up and rushes out of the apartment.

"Have you had breakfast?" I ask Natalia.

"Nope. Wanna get out of here?" she asks me.

I haven't been up to going outside, especially with the paparazzi camping out the front. Firstly, over my story, but secondly, because they have realized Luca and I are dating. I've been working on venturing out with Dr. Regio because he believes I'm ready. But I'm not sure.

"I promise I've got you," Natalia reassures me.

"Sure. I have to join the land of the living sometime, and now sounds like as good a time as any. Did I tell you … no nightmares last night?" I say with a big smile, proud of myself.

"Oh my god." Natalia gives me a huge hug. "I'm so proud of you."

"Thanks. I couldn't have done it without your brother," I tell her.

Natalia rolls her eyes, she's fond of doing that. "He's okay, I guess."

Her comment makes us both burst out in laughter. It's been far too long since I've laughed like that.

35

LILLY

"You did so well." Natalia squeals as we make it back to Luca's apartment, our arms filled with designer bags full of goodies.

"I can't believe I let you talk me into buying all this stuff," I say, staring at the mountains of bags. Never in my life have I spent so much money.

"It's Luca's card, so why not. He can afford it," Natalia says with a shrug.

Natalia sneakily called her brother and explained to him we were going out shopping. He was so excited that I wanted to leave the apartment that he gave her his credit card, assigned us security, and told us to go crazy. She did exactly that, went crazy.

"The total cost of this stuff could feed a small country," I tell her. I feel sick over the amount of money we spent.

"Look, I know you have been thrown into this crazy world and that it's a little more over the top than you're used to …" that's the understatement of the year, "… but I also know how this all works." She turns serious suddenly. "The press can love you one minute, then hate you the next." Natalia reaches out and touches my hand. "You're with Luca now, and that comes with responsibilities and obligations."

"Meaning I have to play my part?" I ask her.

"Not in a bad way," she tries to reassure me. "Just ... one day you will be a future princess."

I hadn't thought that far ahead.

"You know that's where Luca sees it going, don't you?" she adds.

"I've thought about a future with Luca, but I guess I forgot to add in the prince part," I say as I nervously play with my hands.

"You haven't really seen him in prince mode yet." She grins. "I know he's eager to announce to the world that you're dating."

Oh.

"But there's protocol when it comes to that." She rolls her eyes.

"I hope you aren't scaring her," Luca's deep voice echoes through the apartment. "Hey, beautiful." Luca places a kiss on my forehead, then sits down beside us. "Lilly, you're looking a little shell-shocked."

"She keeps forgetting you're a prince." Natalia laughs.

"I haven't really shown you that part of my life, have I?" he says with a chuckle.

Shaking my head, I don't reply. I mean, I have seen the cars, the apartment, the security, and the jet, but not the adoring fans.

"Right, well, that's my cue to leave. Brother ..." Natalia kisses Luca. "Lil ... you did so well today." She hugs me, then she walks out of the apartment with all her bags leaving me with Luca.

"Guess we might need to talk about some things?" he says.

I nod in agreement.

Luca moves over and sits beside me on the sofa. "Well, firstly. I love you."

"Are you softening me up?" I ask with a giggle.

"Yeah, pretty much." He grins, and honestly, it makes me weak. It always does.

"Secondly, I want to spend the rest of my life with you."

That's good to know because I feel the same way.

"When the time is right, I'll be putting a ring on your finger," he states surely.

Oh.

"Thirdly, things will change for you, and I hope you are able to accept them. You will have to give up so much to be with me, and I'm sorry for that."

I can see it on his face, he's worried about my answer. "I love you, Luca." Leaning over, I kiss him. "I want you and only you."

"Do you love me enough to give up practicing medicine, though?" he asks tentatively.

Oh. Okay, now I understand the troubled look.

"Can't I do both?" I ask.

He shakes his head. "Once we're engaged, you'll have to stop. You will have other obligations."

"So, until then, I can?" I question him.

He nods. "If I'm honest, I don't want you to go back to the frontline, Lil."

"Is there a compromise?" I ask.

"You would compromise for me?" He sounds surprised.

As much as I love medicine, and I do with all my heart, I love him more.

"I love you, Luca. I want to be with you. I wouldn't mind doing some medicine on the side, it's a part of me, in whatever form that may be," I tell him honestly.

He excitedly pulls me into his lap. "Consider it done."

"Just like that, hey?" I say with a giggle.

"Kind of ... um ... you realize you'll have to go to princess boot camp?" He chuckles.

"If I can ace medical school, I can ace princess school, can't I?" I question him.

"Princess school is much harder." He chuckles.

Bring it on.

36

LUCA

Two years ago, this crazy brunette stumbled into the cottage I rented and bowled me over instantly, and not because she couldn't take her eyes off my dick, that was a bonus. I could be myself around her—the palaces, the money, the title—it had all been stripped away, and she fell for me anyway. Then there was her. How could I not fall for this genuine, funny, strong, intelligent, beautiful, and totally awkward woman? Now our fairy tale didn't exactly go to plan as we had evil sisters and exes crashing into our lives. We had monsters trying to destroy us. But somehow, we have made it through.

Lilly has really embraced her new life. The people love her, the media thinks she is fantastic, and they love the fact that she's a doctor and not just a socialite on my arm. My parents couldn't be happier, especially when she sneaks my father a little slice of cheese. She's embraced everything her role as future princess entails, and all with a smile on her face. I don't think I could love her any more than I do today.

Lilly's family has tried to make contact, especially now it's been revealed that the two of us are together. But she said, "If they can't be there for me in the worst of times, they sure as hell can't be there for the best of times."

I thought things would change, but she is still standing firm, and I must accept that's the way she wants it.

We went to her sister's wedding back in Glencoe during the summer. It was great being back in the village. They didn't treat me any differently once they found out who I really was. They still gave me warnings that a palace wouldn't protect me if I hurt Lilly, and I have no doubt they would too.

Not long after the wedding, Laura and Andy announced they were having a baby, and if I'm honest, I'm kind of jealous. I can't wait to see Lilly carrying our baby or babies. But first, I need to put this ring on her finger, and then we can plan the rest of our lives together.

I have whisked her away to my villa in the alps. I'm trying to recreate the moment we met. Thought I'd do the full-circle thing. I left earlier than her to set everything up. I came in via helicopter because it's too far to drive for one night. The helicopter is now on its way back to Rome to pick Lilly up as I rush to get everything ready for tonight. I want it to be perfect, and I want her to say yes.

My phone lights up with a text from my helicopter pilot letting me know he has dropped Lilly off, so it shouldn't be long until she arrives.

I'm nervous, like really nervous.

"Babe," Lilly calls out through the empty villa.

I take a deep breath and make my way into the living room where she's standing.

"Oh. My. God," Lilly squeals, then bursts out laughing.

Okay, seeing your partner naked should not make you laugh, especially as this is a special moment.

"Why does your dick have a bow wrapped around it?" she asks.

"Unwrap it and see," I tell her, giving her a seductive wink that makes her bend over laughing. This isn't at all how I thought the evening would go.

She walks over to me, and I notice the tear marks running down her cheeks. But then her hands are on my dick, and I forget all about my humiliation. She's unwrapping the bow, and the box falls to the floor.

That's my cue to get down on one knee.

"Lilly Ava Simpson ..." I start.

"Yes. Yes. Yes," she screams at me before I even get to finish my question.

"Babe, I haven't asked you anything yet."

"Oh, yeah, you're right, continue ..." She smirks.

This is not going to plan, but I power on.

"Lilly, when I look at you, all I see is a long life ahead filled with laughter and happiness." Now, real tears are falling down her cheeks. "There's no one else in this world I want to spend the rest of my life with. Will you marry me?"

The speech I had prepared was so much better than what I just said, but nerves have gotten the better of me. You would think for a prince who does so much public speaking, I could do such a simple speech with ease, but this is Lilly, and she is so much more important than any other speech I have ever made.

"Yes." She rushes me then kisses me. "Yes. Yes. Yes."

"I need to put the ring on."

"Shivers, sorry. I've messed this all up for you. I'm sorry, babe," Lilly apologizes.

"As long as you said yes, that's all that matters," I reply, opening the blue ring box.

"Holy moly." Lilly gasps while I pull out the family heirloom. "That's one big diamond."

I take it out from the velvet box and slide it onto her finger.

"It's so heavy, but I don't care because it's beautiful," she says, admiring it.

"It's over three hundred years old," I tell her.

Lilly's eyes widen.

"Many royals have worn this ring," I explain to her.

"That makes it so much more special. It's like a connection with long-lost family. Knowing that someone wore this a lifetime ago is just wow. I love it, Luca," she says, staring down at it.

My body relaxes. I was unsure whether or not she'd love a second-hand ring, but she does because she understands the family history significance of it.

"I can't wait to spend the rest of my life with you, Principessa Lilly," I say.

"Okay, that part is going to take some getting used to." She giggles while staring at the ring on her finger.

"Hey ..." She stops and looks around the villa, noticing it for the first time. "You told me your friend owned a vineyard in Trento. Is this his place?"

I shake my head. "It's mine, or should I say, ours."

"What? So that bottle of wine you had was from your vineyard, and you never told me?" she asks.

"Honestly, it slipped my mind. I had forgotten all about that," I say.

"Luckily, I'm dazzled by this diamond not to care about your deceitful ways." She chuckles.

I pull her to the ground and roll her on top of me. "I love you, Lilly."

"I love you, Luca," she says as she looks down at me with pure love and adoration in her eyes.

"Can I now take my fiancée upstairs and consummate this engagement?" I ask her.

"Yes, please, Your Highness." Lilly giggles as I carry her through the villa, and I couldn't be happier.

EPILOGUE - LILLY

One year later

"We have good news," Mackenzie tells me on the phone. "We've found Ilona."

"Oh my god." My stomach somersaults over the news. "Is she okay?"

"Yes, she is," she says.

"Where was she?" I wonder what kind of hell she has been through all this time.

"We found her in Dubai," Mackenzie tells me. "A maid smuggled her and the others out. We also rescued the maid and her family for helping us," she explains.

"We can give them refugee status here in Italy. Please, tell them that," I tell her.

"Thank you. Having you and Luca on board helping us rehome these women in a safe and secure commune is …" Mackenzie gets emotional. "You're changing their lives."

"Please, you guys are doing the heavy lifting," I tell her.

Giving up my job as a doctor after marrying Luca was hard. I knew that it wouldn't be easy in a palace as a princess. Thankfully, he understood, and for my wedding present, he gave me one of his farms to me to start my foundation.

Lilly's Place—a village that's dedicated to women who have been saved from human trafficking and are unable to return home to their own countries. We set them up with a home and some land. We bring the rest of their family out to them if possible. We educate them and help get them back onto their feet. We make sure they have the best psychological help they can get to overcome their trauma, with some needing it more than others. We give them a new, safe life. Luca's present to me was the most amazing gift he could've ever given me outside of my currently rounded belly. I can do my humanitarian work while still serving my new country. I never knew life could be this perfect.

"She'll be arriving in Rome tomorrow," Mackenzie tells me.

"I'll be waiting for her. I want to be the first person she sees in her new life."

"She will need a friendly face. I'll see you tomorrow," Mackenzie says as she signs off.

※ ※ ※ ※

"Would you stop it?" Luca says with a smile as his hand rests on my shaking leg.

"I can't help it," I tell him. The baby's giving me a hard kick in the ribs as I rub my belly. "Ouch."

"You okay?" Luca asks as he looks down at me with concern written across his face.

Since I announced I was pregnant, he has upped the protectiveness tenfold.

"He's just kicking me to tell me to calm down. He's just like his papa," I say, giving my gorgeous husband a smirk. Yes, I'm having a boy. A little prince is on his way, and his family couldn't be happier.

Luca reaches out and rests his hand on my expanding belly,

and instantly our baby settles down. Luca looks up at me, and all I can see is the love shining back at me. He leans over and gives me a chaste kiss.

"Seriously, you two are as bad as my sisters with their partners. Always kissing and looking loved up," Mackenzie says, making a gagging face.

"You made it," I say as I slowly get up off the chair and hug her.

"Look at your belly," she says, giving it a quick rub. "You have grown so much since the last time I saw you."

Mackenzie and I have become even closer since all this as have her sisters, Sophie, Zoe, and Grace, and their partners. They are huge advocates for women who have been trafficked as they both were. They were part of the infamous Bratva Jewels, the most elite of the Bratva's arsenal to collect favors. They were used as bribes for high-ranking officials, royalty, ambassadors, police commissioners, and pretty much anyone at the top end of town. Until they were able to escape and one by one take down the Bratva.

"I know. I feel huge," I say as I still have a couple more months to go, and I have no idea how my belly is going to stretch that much more.

"Grace is feeling the same. She's about to pop, too. She moans about not being able to see her feet and blames her partner for getting her in that position." Grace's partner is mysterious, and we haven't been able to meet him, but that's a story for another day.

"They have landed," Mackenzie states as her phone beeps.

My nerves kick in as I watch the plane pull up to a stop. The aerobridge stretches out and joins the plane, obstructing our view of the occupants leaving it. My heart stops for a couple of beats as I wait to see her again. I just hope she's okay.

A couple of bodyguards exit the aerobridge first, and behind them is Ilona. Oh my, she looks so small and frail. That poor girl.

"Ilona," I call out her name.

Those blue eyes look dull and lifeless as she turns and looks over to where I'm standing. The moment she sees me again is when the first spark of color flickers in her eyes.

"Miss Lilly." She cries as she rushes over to me looking like skin and bones. Her spindly arms wrap around me and hold me tight. We both break down.

"You're safe now," I whisper into her neck. "I told you I'd rescue you. I'm so sorry it took me so long."

Ilona shakes her head. "I knew you would come, Miss Lilly. I never gave up hope."

ACKNOWLEDGMENTS

Thanks for finishing this book.
Really hope you enjoyed it.
Why not check out my other books.
Have a fantastic day !

Don't forget to leave a review.
xoxo

ABOUT THE AUTHOR

JA Low lives on the Gold Coast in Australia. When she's not writing steamy scenes and admiring hot surfers, she's tending to her husband and two sons and running after her chickens while dreaming up the next epic romance.

✳✳✳✳

Come follow her

Facebook: www.facebook.com/jalowbooks
TikTok: https://geni.us/vrpoMqH
Instagram: www.instagram.com/jalowbooks
Pinterest: www.pinterest.com/jalowbooks
Website: www.jalowbooks.com
Goodreads: https://www.goodreads.com/author/show/14918059.
J_A_Low
BookBub: https://www.bookbub.com/authors/ja-low

ABOUT THE AUTHOR

Come join JA Low's Block
www.facebook.com/groups/1682783088643205/

✳✳✳✳

JALow Books Website
jalowbooks@gmail.com

Subscribe to her newsletter here

INTERCONNECTING

Bratva Jewels

Book 1 - Sapphire

Book 2 - Diamond

Book 3 - Emerald

ALSO BY JA LOW

The Dirty Texas Box Set

Five full length novels and Five Novellas included in the set.

One band. Five dirty talking rock stars and the women that bring them to their knees.

Wyld & Dirty

A workplace romance with your celebrity hall pass.

Dirty Promises

A best friend to lover's romance with the one man who's off limits.

Bound & Dirty

An opposites attract romance with family loyalty tested to its limits.

Dirty Trouble

A brother's best friend romance with a twist.

Broken & Dirty

A friend's with benefits romance that takes a wild ride.

One little taste can't hurt; can it?

If you like your rock stars dirty talking, alpha's with hearts of gold this series is for you.

ALSO BY JA LOW

Spin off from The Dirty Texas Series

Under the Spanish Sun Series

Hotshot Chef - Book 1

ALSO BY JA LOW

Spin off Dirty Texas Series

Paradise Club Series

Paradise - Book 1

Lost in Paradise - Book 2

Paradise Found - Book 3

Craving Paradise - Book 4

ALSO BY JA LOW

Connected to The Paradise Club

The Art of Love Series

Arrogant Artist - Book 1

ALSO BY JA LOW

Playboys of New York

Off Limits - Book 1

Strictly Forbidden - Book 2

The Merger - Book 3

Taking Control - Book 4

Without Warning - Book 5

ALSO BY JA LOW

Spin off series to Playboys of New York

The Hartford Brothers Series

Book 1 - Tempting the Billionaire

Book 2 - Playing the Player

Book 3 - Seducing the Doctor

Printed in Great Britain
by Amazon